The
Old Capital

by

Yasunari Kawabata

———————

Translated by
J. Martin Holman

NORTH POINT PRESS

San Francisco   1987

Translator's Note

When Kawabata Yasunari won the Nobel Prize in Literature in 1968, *The Old Capital* was one of the three works cited by the committee. The novel was originally serialized in both the Tokyo and Osaka editions of the *Asahi Newspaper* in one hundred installments from October 1961 through January of the following year. As soon as he completed the novel, Kawabata checked himself into the hospital to be treated for an addiction to sleeping medications that he had developed while he was writing the book. Although Kawabata called *The Old Capital* his "abnormal product," the novel takes up familiar themes: recognition of the gulf between the sexes and the anxiety it brings, yearning for the virginal ideal, and the linking of nature and man, setting and character.

The novel is set in Kyoto, a city of high art and the cultural soul of Japan since it became the capital almost eleven hundred years ago. Each obi weaver, kimono designer, tea master, or calligrapher in the ancient city is the recipient of traditions that have been passed down through the ages. Their work embodies not only the peculiar aesthetic sensitivity of the artist himself, but also the spiritual blood of his predecessors as it flows down from the past.

Kawabata himself is often considered a writer who embodies ancient traditions—perhaps the most "Japanese" of modern Japanese authors. (At the same time, many of his techniques and images were avant-garde and even shocking to Japanese readers.) After Japan's defeat in the war, Kawabata said that he would write nothing but elegies for the remaining years of his life, and in *The Old Capital* he laments the decline of old Kyoto in the melancholy tone of elegy, as he depicts the crisis of ambivalence in the traditional artist of post-war Japan; his characters confront disorienting changes that they welcome yet deplore. The novel acknowledges and explores the necessarily ironic, and often seductive, relationship between innovation and tradition—the interplay of passivity and vitality in human existence and human endeavor.

Many friends helped me along the way to completing this translation. I would like to express my appreciation to Steven D. Carter of Brigham Young University, who first introduced me to Japanese literature and the works of Kawabata, to Van C. Gessel of the University of California, Berkeley, whose encouragement and suggestions helped me immensely, and to Hiroko Sugiura and many others who assisted me in deciphering difficult phrases, particularly those in the Kyoto dialect. I am grateful to Tom Ginsberg for bringing North Point Press and me together. I also would like to express my gratitude to Virginia Burnham for typing the manuscript, and to her husband, James Coughlin, for providing a computer for the task. Most of all I want to thank my wife, Susan James Holman, whose patience and endurance in serving as editor, thesaurus, and best friend saw me through to the final draft. I dedicate this translation to her.

J. MARTIN HOLMAN
Berkeley, January 1987

The
Old Capital

The Flowers of Spring

Chieko discovered the violets flowering on the trunk of the old maple tree. "Ah. They've bloomed again this year," she said as she encountered the gentleness of spring.

The maple was rather large for such a small garden in the city; the trunk was larger around than Chieko's waist. But this old tree with its coarse moss-covered bark was not the sort of thing one should compare with a girl's innocent body.

The trunk of the tree bent slightly to the right at about the height of Chieko's waist, and at a height just over her head it twisted even farther. Above the bend the limbs extended outward, dominating the garden, the ends of the longer branches drooping with their own weight.

Just below the large bend were two hollow places with violets growing in each. Every spring they would put forth flowers. Ever since Chieko could remember, the two violets had been there on the tree.

The upper violet and the lower violet were separated by about a foot. "Do the upper and lower violets ever meet? Do they know each other?" Chieko wondered. What could it mean to say that the violets "meet" or "know" one another?

Every spring there were at least three, and sometimes as many as five, buds on the violets in the tiny hollows. Chieko stared at them from the inner corridor that opened onto the garden, lifting her gaze from the base of the trunk of the maple tree. Sometimes she was moved by the "life" of the violets on the tree. Other times their "loneliness" touched her heart.

"To be born in such a place and go on living there . . ."

Though customers who came to the store admired the

splendid maple tree, few noticed the violets blooming on it. The tree had grown strong with age, and the moss on the old trunk gave it dignity and elegance. The tiny violets lodging there attracted no attention.

But the butterflies knew them. Just at the moment Chieko noticed the violets, several small white butterflies came fluttering through the garden near the flowers. Their dancing whiteness shone brightly against the maple, which was just beginning to open its own small red buds.

The flowers and leaves of the two violets cast a faint shadow on the new green of the moss on the maple trunk.

It was a cloudy, soft spring day.

Chieko sat in the corridor looking at the violets on the trunk until the butterflies had passed.

"You've bloomed again for me," Chieko wanted to whisper.

At the base of the maple, just below the violets, stood an old lantern. Chieko's father had once told her that the standing image carved on the pedestal was that of Christ.

"Are you sure it isn't Mary?" Chieko had asked. "The large statue of Mary at Kitano Tenjin Shrine looks just like this one."

"It's Christ," her father said simply. "It's not holding a baby."

"Ah. Of course," Chieko had to agree. Then she asked, "Were there any Christians among our ancestors?"

"No. A gardener or stonecutter probably placed it here. It's not an uncommon sort of lantern."

This Christian lantern had probably been made during the period when the religion had been proscribed. The rough stone was brittle, so the relief carving had been worn down and broken through hundreds of years of wind and rain. It was distinguishable only as a head, body, and legs. Even when new it was probably but a simple carving. The sleeves were long, almost touching the ground. The hands seemed to be folded in prayer, but one could not tell merely from the small bulge at the forearm. Still, the impression was different from that of the statues of Buddha or the guardian deities.

Whether this Christian lantern had once been a symbol of faith or was nothing more than an ancient exotic ornament, it now stood at the foot of the old maple in the garden of Chieko's family's shop simply for the sake of its antique elegance. If it happened to catch a customer's eye, Chieko's father would tell him that it was a statue of Christ. But few of the salesmen who came noticed the somber lantern in the shade of the great maple tree. Even when someone happened to see it, he never looked at it closely; a lantern or two in a garden is to be expected.

Chieko lowered her gaze from the violets on the tree and looked at the Christ. Although she had not attended a mission school, she had gone to church and read the Old and New Testaments in order to become familiar with English. But she felt the weathered lantern was unworthy to offer flowers or votive candles to; there was no cross carved anywhere on it.

She sometimes thought of the violets above the carving of Christ as the heart of Mary. Once again Chieko lifted her eyes from the lantern to the flowers. Suddenly, she recalled the bell crickets she had been raising in a jar.

Chieko had begun raising bell crickets long after she had first found the violets on the old maple tree. It had been four or five years ago. She had heard them chirping in the parlor of the home of one of her school friends, and had received several as a gift.

"The poor things, living in a jar . . . ," Chieko had said. But her friend had answered that it was better than keeping them in a cage and letting them die there. She said that there were even temples that raised them in large quantities and sold the eggs. It seemed there were many who had similar tastes.

This year, Chieko's bell crickets had increased in number.

She had two jars. Every year about the first of July the eggs would hatch, and about the middle of August the crickets began to chirp. But they were born, chirped, laid eggs, and died all inside of a dark cramped jar. Still, since it preserved the species it was perhaps better than raising one short generation in a cage. But the crickets spent their entire lives in a jar; it was the whole world to them. Chieko had heard the ancient Chinese legend of a "universe in a jar" in which there was a palace in a jar filled with fine wine and delicacies from both land and sea. Isolated from the vulgar world, it was a separate realm, an enchanted land. The story was one of many such legends of wizards and magic.

Of course the bell crickets had not entered the jar because they had renounced the world. Perhaps they did not realize where they were, so they went on living.

What surprised Chieko most about the bell crickets was that if she happened not to put in males from elsewhere, the insects that hatched were stunted and feeble, the result of inbreeding. To prevent that, cricket fanciers would often trade male crickets. Now it was spring and the bell crickets would not begin to chirp until late summer. Still there was some connection between the crickets and the violets blooming in the hollows of the maple tree.

Chieko had placed the bell crickets in the jar herself, but why had the violets come to live in such a cramped spot? The violets bloomed, and this year, too, the crickets would hatch and begin their chirping.

"A natural life . . ."

A gentle breeze teased at Chieko's hair, so she tucked the strands behind her ear. She thought of herself in comparison to the violets and the bell crickets.

"And me . . ."

Chieko was the solitary observer of the tiny violets on this spring day, a day that swelled with the vitality of nature.

The sounds from the shop indicated that someone was leaving for lunch. It was almost time for Chieko to get ready to go out to view the cherry blossoms.

Mizuki Shin'ichi had called Chieko the day before to invite her to see the cherry blossoms at Heian Shrine. A school friend of Shin'ichi had been working as a ticket taker at the entrance to the shrine garden for about two weeks. Shin'ichi heard from this friend that the flowers were now at their peak.

"It seems he's been on the lookout. I don't suppose you can be more certain," Shin'ichi laughed softly. His laugh was charming.

"Is he going to be watching us, too?" Chieko asked.

"He's the gatekeeper, isn't he? He lets anyone in," Shin'ichi laughed again briskly. "But, if you don't like the idea, we could go in separately and meet somewhere inside the garden under the trees. You can look at the blossoms all you want by yourself. They aren't the sort of flowers you can tire of."

"If that's true, why don't you go see them alone?"

"I would, but don't blame me if there's a big rainstorm tonight and the blossoms all get blown off the trees . . . "

"Then we could see how elegant the flowers can look on the ground."

"You think the elegance of fallen flowers has something to do with their lying rain-soaked and muddy on the ground? My impression of fallen flowers is . . . "

"Don't be perverse."

"Who, me?"

Chieko left the house wearing an inconspicuous kimono.

The Heian Shrine was well known for the Festival of Ages. The shrine was built in 1895, the twenty-eighth year of the reign of Emperor Meiji, in honor of Emperor Kanmu, who had established the Heian capital in Kyoto a thousand years earlier, so the shrine hall was not very old. The gate and outer worship hall were said to be modeled after the Otemmon and Great Hall of State of the original Heian capital. A traditional Orange Tree of the Right and a Cherry Tree of the Left were also planted there. Komei, who had been emperor before the capital was moved to Tokyo, was also enshrined there in 1938. Many weddings were held at the altar of the shrine.

The groups of red weeping cherry trees that dressed the garden were one of the splendid sights of Kyoto. "Surely there is nothing that represents the old capital better than these flowers."

As Chieko entered the shrine garden, the color of the weeping cherries blossomed deep in her heart. "Again this year, I've greeted the spring in the capital." She stopped and gazed all about.

Was Shin'ichi waiting somewhere, or had he not yet come? Chieko looked for him, then decided to take in the flowers. She walked down between the blossoming trees to the lawn below. Shin'ichi lay there with his hands folded behind his head. His eyes were closed.

Chieko had not expected to find Shin'ichi asleep. She thought it disgusting that he was napping when he was supposed to be waiting for a young woman. Chieko felt more revulsion at the sight of Shin'ichi sleeping than embarrassment at his bad manners. In her world, Chieko was not accustomed to seeing a man asleep.

At his university, Shin'ichi had probably had many lively discussions with his friends while relaxing on the lawn, looking up at the sky or leaning on his elbows. He had merely adopted the same posture today.

Four or five old women were having a casual conversation beside Shin'ichi, spreading out their lunch on the lawn. Perhaps feeling an affinity for the women, he had sat down beside them and fallen asleep. Thinking that might have been what happened, Chieko almost smiled, but instead she blushed.

She just stood there without calling to wake him. Then Chieko started to walk away from Shin'ichi; she had never looked into the face of a sleeping man.

Shin'ichi was dressed in his school uniform and his hair was all in place. His long eyelashes reminded her of a little boy. Still, she could not look at him directly.

"Chieko," Shin'ichi stood up, calling to her. Chieko felt offended.

"Sleeping in a place like this. It's unseemly. Everyone can see you."

"I wasn't sleeping. I knew when you came."

"You're mean."

"What would you have done if I hadn't called to you?"

"Did you pretend to be asleep when you saw me?"

"I thought, what a happy girl has entered the garden, and I felt sad. And my head has been hurting . . . "

"Me? I'm happy?"

Shin'ichi did not answer.

"You have a headache?"

"No, it feels better."

"Your color is bad."

"No, I'm all right," Shin'ichi protested.

"Your face is like a fine sword."

Shin'ichi had occasionally been told that by others, but this was the first time he had heard it from Chieko.

When something violent within him was about to ignite, people spoke of Shin'ichi's face in such terms.

"Fine swords don't kill people. Besides, we're beneath the flowers here."

Chieko returned to the corridor entrance at the top of a small hill. Shin'ichi stood up and followed her.

"Do you want to see all the flowers before we go?" Chieko asked. At the entrance to the west corridor the blossoms of the red weeping cherry trees suddenly made one feel spring had indeed come. The scarlet double flowers were blooming all the way to the tips of the slenderest weeping branches. It would be more fitting to say that the flowers were borne upon the twigs than to say they were simply blossoming there.

"These are my favorite flowers in the garden," Chieko said, leading Shin'ichi to a place where the corridor turned outward. The branches of a single cherry tree spread particularly wide. Shin'ichi stood beside Chieko, gazing at the tree.

"If you look closely it seems feminine," he said. "The slender drooping branches and the flowers are gentle and lush."

The faintest touch of lavender seemed to reflect on the scarlet of the flowers.

"Until now, I hadn't realized it would be so feminine," Shin'ichi said, "the color of the blossoms, their elegance, their captivating charm . . . "

Leaving the cherry tree, the two of them walked toward the pond. At a narrow spot in the path, where folding stools had been set out and a red carpet spread on the ground, visitors sat drinking tea.

A girl called Chieko's name. Dressed in a formal long-sleeved kimono, Masako came out of the tearoom, the Choshintei, which was in the shadow of the trees.

"Chieko, would you lend a hand for a moment? I'm so tired. I need some help with my teacher's guests."

"Dressed like this, the most I could do is work in the kitchen."

"I don't mind. That would be fine. We're making the tea in the back today."

"I'm with someone."

Noticing Shin'ichi, Masako whispered in Chieko's ear, "Your fiancé?"

Chieko shook her head slightly.

"Boyfriend?"

She shook her head again.

Shin'ichi turned and started to walk away.

"Why don't you come inside and sit down . . . together," Masako suggested. "The place is empty now." But Chieko refused and followed after Shin'ichi.

"She's pretty, isn't she?" Chieko asked when she caught up with Shin'ichi.

"An ordinary sort of pretty," he responded.

"Oh, she might hear you."

Chieko nodded to Masako, who waved good-bye.

The path below the tearoom came out at a pond. Near the bank, the leaves of the water irises stood vying with one another in their youthful green. Water-lily pads floated on the surface of the pond.

There were no cherry trees here.

Walking around the bank, Chieko and Shin'ichi entered a small path in the shadow of some trees. It smelled of young leaves and damp earth. The narrow shaded path was short; where it ended, a bright garden opened up beside a pond that was larger than the previous one. The flowers of the red weeping cherry trees were reflected in the water and flashed in the eyes of the visitors. Some foreign tourists were photographing the blossoms.

But on the opposite bank in a grove of trees, an andromeda tree modestly put forth its white blossoms. Chieko thought of the old city of Nara. There were also pine trees that were well shaped, but not tall. Had there been no cherry blossoms, the green of the pines would still remain to catch the eye. No, even now the undefiled green of the pines and the water in the pond enlivened the masses of red weeping cherry blossoms.

Shin'ichi walked on ahead and crossed the stepping-stones in the pond, which were known as "marsh-crossing" stones. They were round like the columns of a Shinto gate that had been sliced and lined up across the pond. In spots, Chieko had to lift her kimono a bit to cross.

Shin'ichi glanced back at her.

"I wish I could carry you across."

"I'd be impressed . . . if you could."

Even an old woman could cross these stepping-stones.

Water-lily leaves floated on the water around the stones. As Chieko and Shin'ichi approached the bank, the small pines were reflected in the pond.

"I wonder if the way these stepping-stones are placed represents some sort of abstraction," Shin'ichi said.

"Aren't all Japanese gardens abstract? Like the moss among the cedars in the garden at Daigoji Temple. But the more everyone talks about how 'abstract' it is, the more distasteful it becomes."

"That's true. The moss on those cedar trees is surely abstract. They've finished repairs on the pagoda at Daigoji. Would you like to see it? . . . the unveiling?"

"Has it been rebuilt like the new Gold Pavilion?"

"It's probably been newly painted. The pagoda didn't burn down like the Gold Pavilion. They took it apart, then reassembled it as it was originally. The unveiling will be when the flowers are at their best. There should be crowds of people there."

"I don't care to see any flowers besides these cherry blossoms here."

The two crossed the last of the stepping-stones to the inner side of the garden and reached the bank where a group of pines stood. Then Chieko and Shin'ichi went on to the Bridge Hall. Correctly, it was the Soheikaku, but it was actually a bridge that looked like a hall. Both sides of the bridge resembled low benches with arm rests. People sat there to relax and admire the layout of the garden. Some of the people seated there were taking refreshments, while children ran about the center of the bridge.

"Shin'ichi! Shin'ichi! Over here . . . " Chieko took a seat, putting down her right hand to save a place for him.

"I'll stand," Shin'ichi said. "Or maybe I'll just squat here at your feet."

"No, you won't." Chieko stood up quickly and forced Shin'ichi to sit down. "I'll go buy some food for the carp."

Chieko returned and tossed food into the pond. Scrambling for it, the carp piled on top of each other. Some even came up out of the water. The rings of waves spread outward, causing the reflections of the cherries and pines to tremble in the pond.

"Would you like to throw in the rest?" she asked Shin'ichi, holding out the remaining food.

Shin'ichi said nothing.

"Does your head still hurt?"

"No."

They sat for a long while. Shin'ichi stared closely at the surface of the water, his face clear.

"What are you thinking about?" Chieko asked.

"Hmm . . . I wonder myself. Aren't there times when you're happy just thinking of nothing?"

"Of course. On days like this with the flowers."

"No. I mean in the company of such a happy girl. Your happiness drifts on the breeze like a fragrance."

"Am I happy?" Chieko asked. A shadow of melancholy flickered across her face. But she was looking down, so it may have been just the pond water reflecting in her eyes.

Chieko stood up. "There's a cherry tree I like on the other side of the bridge."

"I can see it. It's that one, isn't it?"

The tree was a splendid sight, famous for its branches, which drooped like a weeping willow, yet spread out wide. As Chieko stood beside the tree, flower petals fell about her feet and shoulders in the delicate breeze.

The flowers lay scattered on the ground. A few petals floated on the pond as well, but no more than seven or eight.

The tree was supported by a bamboo scaffolding, but it seemed as if the delicate tips of its branches would touch the ground. Beyond the pond, above the groves of trees on the east bank, the mountains with their new young leaves were visible through the blossoms of the double cherry.

"Is that part of Higashiyama?" asked Shin'ichi.

"It's Daimonjiyama," Chieko answered.

"Really? Daimonjiyama? Doesn't it look awfully tall?"

"That's because you're looking at it from beneath the flowers." So saying, Chieko joined Shin'ichi under the blossoming tree.

They were reluctant to leave.

Coarse white sand was spread around the cherry tree. A group of beautiful pines, rather tall for this garden, stood to the right. Beside them was the exit to the shrine garden.

As they passed through the gate, Chieko said, "I want to go to Kiyomizu."

"Kiyomizu Temple?" Shin'ichi's face betrayed his lack of interest.

"I'd like to see the sunset over the capital from Kiyomizu, to watch the sun go down in the sky over Nishiyama," Chieko said.

Shin'ichi nodded. "Let's go."

"Shall we walk?"

The road was rather long. They avoided the trains, taking the more distant route around to Nanzenji Temple Road, passing behind Chianji Temple. Then they passed through the rear of Maruyama Park, walking the old narrow path to Kiyomizu Temple.

The only sightseers left on the veranda of the temple were a few girl students, but their faces were not clearly visible.

This was the hour Chieko had come to prefer. Votive candles were burning in the dark recesses of the Great Hall, but Chieko passed by without stopping, walking on from the Amida Hall to the rear sanctuary.

The veranda of the rear sanctuary was built overhanging a cliff. Like the light, buoyant, cypress bark roof, the veranda, too, appeared to be delicately suspended. The veranda faced west, looking out over the capital toward Nishiyama.

The lights burning in the city cast a faint glow over the town.

Chieko leaned against the railing and gazed toward the west. She seemed to have forgotten about Shin'ichi. He drew near to her.

"Shin'ichi. I was an abandoned child, a foundling," Chieko spoke abruptly.

"An abandoned child?"

"Yes."

Shin'ichi puzzled over whether the words "abandoned child" had some psychological meaning.

"Abandoned," Shin'ichi whispered. "Do you sometimes feel as though you were an abandoned child? If you are abandoned, so am I . . . spiritually. Maybe all people are abandoned children. Perhaps birth is like being abandoned on earth by God."

Shin'ichi stared at Chieko's profile. The glow of dusk colored her cheeks ever so faintly. Perhaps it was the poignancy of the spring evening.

"They do say we are God's children. He abandons us here, then saves us. . . . "

But Chieko looked down on the lights of the old capital city as if she heard nothing. She did not even turn to Shin'ichi.

Sensing an incomprehensible sadness within Chieko, Shin'-ichi started to put his hand on her shoulder. She pulled away.

"You shouldn't touch an abandoned child."

"But I said God's children, all people, are abandoned here," Shin'ichi raised his voice.

"It's nothing so complicated as that. I wasn't abandoned by God. My human parents abandoned me."

Shin'ichi did not speak.

"I was a foundling, left in front of the Bengara lattice door of the shop."

"What are you talking about?"

"It's true. I can't help it. I wanted to tell you. When I stand here on the veranda of Kiyomizu, looking out on the sunset over this huge city, I wonder if I was born here in Kyoto."

"What are you talking about? You're crazy."

"Why would I lie about something like this?"

"Because you're the pampered only child of a wholesaler. An only daughter is a slave to her delusions."

"My parents do love and care for me. It doesn't matter now that I was a foundling."

"Do you have proof that you were a foundling?"

"Proof? The lattice door. I know that old door well." Chieko's voice became more lovely. "I was in middle school, I think, when my mother called me to her and said I was not her own daughter, not one who caused her the pain of childbirth. She said they stole me as a baby and escaped in a car. But mother and father have different stories about where they got me. Sometimes they say it was in the evening beneath the cherry blossoms at the Gion Shrine. Other times it's the Kamo riverbed. They think it would be too painful for me to know I was abandoned in front of the shop."

"Do you know who your real parents are?"

"The parents I have now love me very much. I don't have any desire to look for my real mother and father. Perhaps they are even among the Buddhas of the potter's field in Adashino. Of course, the stones there are quite old."

The soft evening color of spring had spread, like a faint red mist, from Nishiyama across half the sky.

Shin'ichi could not believe that Chieko was a foundling, much less a kidnapped child. Chieko's home was in an old wholesaler's neighborhood, so asking around, one could know if what she said was true. Naturally, Shin'ichi did not want to investigate. He was puzzled. Why had Chieko made such a confession to him?

Had she led him here to Kiyomizu just to reveal this to him? Chieko's voice had become pure, and in its depths ran a beautiful note of strength. She had not seemed to be appealing to Shin'ichi. Surely Chieko vaguely realized that Shin'ichi loved her. Was her confession meant to reveal her heart to the one she loved? It did not sound that way to Shin'ichi. Rather, it echoed of a rejection of his love, even if she had simply made up the story about being a foundling.

At Heian Shrine, Shin'ichi had repeated several times that Chieko was "happy." Thinking she might be protesting that, he spoke. "After you realized that you were a foundling, were you sad? Did you feel forsaken?"

"No, not in the least. Only when I told my father I wanted to go to college, and he said it would just get in the way since I am to succeed to the family business, only then did I ever feel sadness."

"Was that last year?"

"Yes."

"Are you completely obedient to your parents?"

"Yes, completely."

"Even when it comes to something like marriage?"

"Yes. I intend to be." Chieko answered without hesitation.

"What about yourself? Don't you have your own feelings?" Shin'ichi asked.

"It seems to cause trouble when one has too many."

"So you suppress them . . . you stifle your feelings completely?"

"No, not that."

"You're speaking nothing but riddles." Shin'ichi tried to laugh lightly, but his voice faltered. Leaning forward on the railing, he gazed at Chieko.

"I want to look at the face of a puzzling abandoned child."

"It's already dark now." Chieko turned toward Shin'ichi for the first time. Her eyes flashed as she looked up at the roof of the Great Hall. "How frightening," she cried out.

The cypress roof seemed to press down ominously with a ponderous dark mass.

The Convent Temple
and the Lattice Door

Three or four days earlier, Chieko's father, Sada Takichiro, had secluded himself in a temple hidden deep in a remote part of Saga.

It was a convent temple and the head abbess of the hermitage was more than sixty-five years old. The small convent was historic because of its association with the old capital, but it was a quiet temple. The entrance was hidden by a grove of bamboo, so tourists seldom visited. Not being well known, the detached room of the temple was used only infrequently for a tea ceremony. On occasion, the abbess left the convent to teach flower arranging.

Could one say that Sada Takichiro had come to resemble this temple, where he rented a room?

Sada's business was a wholesale dry goods shop in the Nakagyo Ward of Kyoto. He had incorporated his shop as had most others around him. Takichiro was, of course, the president, but he left the transactions to his clerks. Still, he did retain many business practices reminiscent of a traditional shop.

Since his youth, Takichiro had had the disposition of a master. He disliked people. He utterly lacked the ambition to hold a one-man show of his weaving and dyeing work, but they would not have sold even if he had displayed them, for they were too novel.

His father Takichibei quietly observed his son's actions. The shop did not lack for stylish designs, as it handled patterns drawn by its own designer and other artists. But when Takichibei realized that his son, who was no genius, had hit a slump and started producing queer designs under the influence of narcotics, he had sent him straight to the hospital.

After Takichiro took over the shop, his designs became more normal, and this he lamented. His reason for shutting himself up alone in the convent was to obtain a heavenly design.

Kimono styles had changed markedly since the war. Takichiro recalled the strange, narcotic-inspired designs of his early years, and wondered if now they might not be considered refreshingly abstract, but he was already in his late fifties.

"Shall I go with a bold classic pattern?" Takichiro sometimes whispered to himself, but his mind was flooded with scores of superb patterns from earlier days. All the patterns and colors of ancient cloth filled his head. Naturally, he also walked through the famous parks, mountains, and fields of Kyoto making sketches for kimonos.

Chieko came about noon.

"Father, would you like some Morika boiled tofu? I bought some for you."

"Oh, thank you. I'm glad you brought the tofu, but I'm even more pleased that you've come. Won't you stay until evening and help unravel the thoughts in this old head . . . so I can think up a good design?"

A cloth wholesaler does not need to draw patterns. Such a pursuit can, in fact, get in the way of business. But Takichiro sometimes sat for as long as half a day at his desk by a secluded parlor window, facing the inner garden and its Christian lantern. Behind the desk in two old paulownia-wood wardrobes were samples of ancient Chinese and Japanese cloth. The bookcases to the sides of them were filled with patterns of fabrics from around the world.

On the second floor of a storage shed, separated from the

shop, were a number of Noh theatre costumes and wedding kimonos preserved in their original state. There was also a great deal of chintz from the South Seas.

He had inherited some items from his father and grand-father, but when exhibitions of ancient cloth were held and a display was requested of him, Takichiro would flatly decline. "According to the wishes of my father, the cloth doesn't leave this house." He was stubborn in his refusal.

The Sada house was an old-style Kyoto home, so one had to pass through the narrow hall beside Takichiro's desk to reach the bathroom. He would frown silently at those comings and goings, but when the shop became noisy, he would call out sharply, "Can't you be quiet?"

The clerk would bow low to the floor. "We have a customer from Osaka."

"It's fine with me if he doesn't buy anything here. There are other wholesalers."

"But he's an old steady customer."

"One buys fabrics with the eye. If he has to use his mouth, surely he must have no sense for them. A real businessman would know at a glance. But, then . . . we do have a lot of cheap stuff here, too."

"Yes, sir."

Takichiro had an antique foreign carpet spread on the floor from his desk to his cushion, and draperies of fine southern chintz surrounded him. This had been Chieko's idea. The draperies softened the noise from the store. From time to time Chieko changed them for a new pattern, and when she did so, Takichiro realized the gentleness of her heart. He spoke to her of Java or Persia, of some period of history or the design of the cloth of the draperies. Chieko did not always understand his detailed explanations.

"This is too good to use for bags and too big to cut up for tea wrappers. If you made it into obi sashes, how many could you cut from it?" Chieko asked once as she looked around at the chintz fabric enclosing her father's workplace.

"Bring me those scissors," her father said.

Takichiro cut the chintz drapes with the expertise one would expect of him.

"This will make a good obi for you, won't it, Chieko?"

Chieko was startled. Tears welled in her eyes. "Oh, no, Father."

"It's all right. It's all right. If you would wear an obi made from this chintz maybe some new ideas for designs would come to me again."

That was the obi Chieko wore to the temple in Saga.

Of course, Takichiro noticed the chintz obi immediately, but did not give it a second look. The pattern was large and showy for a chintz design, with both dark and pale areas. He had wondered how it would look on a girl Chieko's age.

Chieko placed a lunch box at her father's side.

"Will you have something to eat? Wait just a moment, I'll prepare the tofu for you."

Her father was silent.

Chieko stood up and turned toward the bamboo grove by the gate.

"It's already 'bamboo autumn,'" her father said. "The earthen walls here have started to crumble and lean. They've all but collapsed . . . just like me."

Chieko was accustomed to hearing her father speak in such a manner. She did not even try to console him. She merely repeated his words, "bamboo autumn."

"How do the cherry trees look along the way here?" her father asked casually.

"The fallen petals are floating on the pond. And there are a couple of trees still in bloom on the mountain among the new green leaves of the other trees. They're all the more lovely from a distance as you walk by."

Chieko went into the kitchen. Takichiro could hear the sound of her chopping onions and grating dried fish. She returned after putting away the utensils she had used to prepare the meal. Takichiro had brought enough dishes from home for his stay.

Chieko waited on her father piously.

"Why don't you have some with me?" her father asked.

"Thank you," Chieko answered.

Takichiro looked his daughter over from her shoulder to her waist. "It's so drab. You always wear my designs. You're probably the only person who does. You always end up wearing what won't sell."

"It's all right. I wear them because I like them."

"Hmm. They're so plain."

"They *are* plain, but . . ."

"There's nothing wrong with a young girl wearing plain clothes," Chieko's father spoke with unexpected severity.

"People who examine it closely always compliment me."

Takichiro now drew designs merely as a hobby or diversion. The shop had become a wholesale business aimed at popular tastes, so the head clerk would never produce more than two or three of each of Takichiro's patterns, in order to save face for the master. Chieko would always wear them willingly. The fabric for her clothing was carefully selected.

"It's not necessary that you wear only my designs," Takichiro said. "And you don't have to wear kimonos just from our shop, either. You needn't feel such an obligation."

"Obligation?" Chieko was taken aback. "I don't wear them out of obligation."

"If you start wearing showy kimonos, should I assume you've found yourself a man?" Her father laughed loudly, but he did not smile.

As she was serving the boiled tofu, Chieko noticed her father's great desk. There was nothing here to indicate that he had been designing a dye pattern, only an Edo-period lacquer inkstone box and two rolls of reproductions of Koya fabric that rested on one corner.

Chieko wondered if her father had come to the temple to forget about the business at the shop.

"It's never too late to learn, so I'm studying calligraphy," Takichiro spoke with some embarrassment. "But the flowing line of these Fujiwara characters will probably be of some use to me in my designs."

Chieko was silent.

"It's miserable. My hand trembles so."

"What if you drew them larger?"

"I am already drawing large characters."

"What's that rosary on top of the inkstone box?"

"Oh, that? I asked the abbess for it. She gave it to me."

"Do you use it to worship?"

"It's what young people nowadays might call my 'mascot.' But sometimes I feel like cracking the beads with my teeth."

"What a nasty idea. I imagine it's stained with years of fingerprints."

"What do you mean 'nasty'? They're the fingerprints of the faith of generations of nuns."

Feeling as though she had touched a sorrow in her father, Chieko silently lowered her eyes. She carried the dishes of leftover food back to the kitchen.

"Where is the abbess?" Chieko asked when she returned.

"She'll probably be back soon. What are you going to do?"

"I'm going to take a walk around Saga, then go home. There are probably crowds of people at Arashiyama now, but I also like Nonomiya, Adashino, and the path to Nison'in Temple, so I'll go there."

"If you like places like that at your age, I can imagine what you'll be like when you're old. Don't take after me!" Takichiro said.

"Is it possible for a woman to take after a man?"

Chieko's father stood on the veranda, watching her as she walked away.

The old abbess soon returned and began cleaning the garden.

Takichiro sat at his desk. He called to mind the paintings of ferns and flowers by Sotatsu and Korin. He thought of Chieko, who had just left.

The convent where Takichiro had secluded himself was hidden from the village road by a grove of bamboo. To visit the Nembutsuji Temple of Adashino, Chieko climbed the ancient steps as far as the two stone Buddhas on the cliff to the left, but hearing the sound of chattering voices coming from farther ahead, she stopped.

The countless hundreds of dilapidated stone pillars there were called Buddhas of the potter's field. Nowadays, photography sessions were occasionally held there; women dressed in unusual, thin kimonos would be posed among the stones of the small toppled pillars. Today, the voices were probably from such a gathering.

Chieko descended the stone steps from the Buddhist statues, recalling her father's words. Even if her reason for going to Adashino was merely to avoid the spring tourists at Arashiyama, such places as Adashino and Nonomiya were certainly not appropriate for a young girl to visit, less suitable even than wearing her father's drab kimono designs.

"Father doesn't appear to be doing anything at that old temple." Chieko felt a faint sadness pierce her chest. "I wonder what he could be thinking about as he sits biting on those old, grimy rosary beads."

Chieko knew how, in the shop, her father would often try to stifle the sound of biting on a rosary—so violently, it seemed he might crush the beads with his teeth.

"It would be better if he bit my finger," Chieko whispered, shaking her head. Then she turned her thoughts to the time when she and her mother struck the bell at the Nembutsuji Temple together. The bell tower had been newly built. Her mother was a small woman, so try though she would, the bell made little sound, but Chieko put her hand on her mother's and taking a deep breath, they struck the bell together. It resounded loudly.

"We did it! I wonder how far it will echo." Her mother was elated.

"Not as far as when the priest strikes it. He's experienced," Chieko laughed.

Chieko recalled that incident as she walked the lane toward Nonomiya. A notice along the way read, "This path passes through a deep bamboo thicket." The sign was not very old, but what once may have been a dark footpath was now bright and open. There was even a vendor in front of the gate who called to Chieko.

The small shrine, however, had not changed. It was described even in the *Tale of Genji*. The imperial princesses who were to serve at Ise Shrine would spend three years here purifying themselves from the unclean world before going on to Ise. The shrine was known for its small brushwood fence and its Shinto gate made of wood with the bark still attached.

The road through the fields ran from the front of Nonomiya, opening out on the expanse of Arashiyama.

Chieko boarded a bus by a row of pines on the near side of Watatsuki Bridge.

"I wonder what I should tell Mother. She'll suspect something is wrong with Father."

Many of the houses in Nakagyo were lost in the Teppo Fire

and the Dondon Fire, before the Meiji Restoration. Takichiro's shop had not escaped damage.

Although there were old Kyoto-style houses left with lattice doors and lattice windows in the second story, none was more than one hundred years old. The storage room behind the shop, however, was said to have survived the fires.

The shop had not been refurbished in a modern style. That was partly due to the temperament of the master, but it may also have been the fault of the spiritless wholesale business.

Returning home, Chieko opened the lattice door and looked through to the rear of the house. Her mother, Shige, was sitting at Takichiro's desk smoking a cigarette. She propped her cheek on her left hand, and her back was bent as if she were reading or writing, but there was nothing on the desk.

"I'm home." Chieko approached her mother.

"Oh, thank you for your help." Shige seemed to come to herself. "How's your father?"

"Well. . . ," Chieko groped for an answer. "I bought some tofu for him."

"The Morika kind? He was probably very pleased. Was it boiled?"

Chieko nodded.

"How was Arashiyama?" her mother asked.

"Crowds of people were out today."

"Did your father go with you to Arashiyama?"

"No, the abbess was out, so he had to stay to look after the place." Then Chieko thought of an answer. "Father seems to be studying calligraphy."

"Calligraphy?" Her mother spoke as if it were nothing extraordinary. "I hope learning calligraphy will calm his heart. I studied it once, too."

Chieko looked at her mother's noble face and fair complexion. There was no movement that Chieko could read in her countenance.

"Chieko," her mother called softly. "Chieko, when the time comes, you don't have to take over the shop." Chieko did not respond, so Shige continued, "If you want, you may marry into another family and leave home."

Still, Chieko was silent.

"Are you listening to me?"

"Why are you talking about such things?"

"I can't tell you in a word, but I'm fifty years old now. I've thought about what to say for some time."

"What if you and Father just gave up the business and retired, Mother?" Chieko's beautiful eyes moistened.

"We don't have to make that big a jump, but . . ." Chieko's mother smiled slightly.

"Chieko, you said we should quit the business. Is that what you really think?" Her mother's voice was not loud, but she seemed to turn on her daughter. Or had Chieko imagined the smile on her mother's face?

"That's how I feel," Chieko answered. A thread of pain passed through her chest.

"I'm not angry. Please don't make such a face. You know who would be the sadder, the young girl who can say her parents should quit their work, or the old woman who hears her say it."

"Mother, please forgive me."

"It's not a question of whether I forgive you or not."

Then her mother really smiled. "That doesn't sound like what I said a bit ago, does it?"

"I don't understand what I would say myself."

"People . . . especially women, can change what they say."

"Mother."

"Did you tell your father the same thing at Saga?"

"No. I haven't said anything to father."

"Tell him and see what he says . . . please. He's a man and he'll probably be angry, but I'm certain that he'll be pleased in his heart." Her mother rested her forehead on her hand. "I was sitting here at the desk thinking about your father."

"Mother, you know what's happening, don't you?"

"What do you mean?"

The mother and daughter were silent for a while. Then Chieko spoke, as if she could not keep still. "Shall I go to Nishiki to get something for dinner?"

"Yes, please."

Chieko stood up and went toward the shop, stepping down onto the earthen floor of the entry room. Originally, the room had been narrow, extending far to the back. On the wall opposite the shop, black stoves stood in a row. This had been the kitchen.

Now, of course, the stoves were no longer used. A gas range had been installed in the back of the entry room and a wood floor had been put in, but the lower portion was the original plaster, so the draftiness made the severe winters of Kyoto particularly bitter.

The hearth, however, was still intact, probably because faith in Kojin, the fire god of the hearth, was still common. A Shinto talisman was hung behind the fireplace as a precaution against fire. Potbellied statues of Hotei, the god of fortune, also stood in a row. There were seven now, but the number increased each year when the Sadas bought one at the Inari Shrine in Fushimi on the Hatsuuma in February. If there were a death in the family, they would remove the figures and begin again with one.

Seven figures of gods stood on the hearth in the shop; there had been no deaths for seven, even ten years.

A white porcelain vase was placed to the side of the row of

gods on the hearth. Every two or three days, Chieko's mother would sprinkle water on the shelf and carefully wipe it.

Just as Chieko was preparing to go out shopping with her basket in hand, she saw a young man about to enter the lattice door.

"It's the man from the bank," she called to her mother.

He had not noticed Chieko.

There was nothing to worry about; it was the same young bank employee who always came. But Chieko's feet grew heavy when she drew close to the lattice door in front of the shop. As she walked, she ran her fingers along each strip of lattice work.

On reaching the street, Chieko glanced back at the shop, then looked up. The old signboard in front of the lattice window on the second floor caught her eye. The small roof attached to the sign was the mark of a shop of old standing, but it also seemed to be a sort of decoration.

The inclining sun of the peaceful spring shone on the dull weatherworn lettering of the sign, making it look all the more forlorn. The thick cotton shop-door curtain was faded white, with heavy threads dangling from it.

"Even the red weeping cherries at Heian Shrine have times when they are lonely, subdued by this kind of feeling." Chieko hurried away.

People were crowded about Nishiki market as always.

On her way back to the shop, Chieko saw a Shirakawa woman and called to her, "Please stop by our house, too."

"I will, thank you. Are you on your way home?" the woman asked. "Where have you been?"

"To Nishiki. I'd also like to buy some flowers from you for the family altar."

"Oh. Thank you. See if there's anything you'd like."

The "flowers" were actually branches of *sakaki* like those used in Shinto rituals, and on the branches were young leaf buds.

The Shirakawa women came around on the first and fifteenth of each month.

"I'm so glad you were home today," the Shirakawa woman said.

Choosing a small branch of tender buds made Chieko's heart beat faster. Grasping the *sakaki* branch in one hand, she entered the house. "Mother, I'm home." Her voice was bright.

Chieko opened the lattice door again halfway and looked out at the street. The Shirakawa woman was still there.

"Please come in and rest a while before you go. I'll make some tea," Chieko called to her.

"Thank you. You're always so kind." The woman nodded. Then carrying her flowers over her head she stepped into the entry room. "All I brought is some plain field flowers."

"I like field flowers. Thank you for remembering." Chieko gazed at the flowers gathered from meadows and mountains.

Just inside the gate beside the hearth was an old well with a woven bamboo cover. Chieko placed the *sakaki* and flowers on it.

"I'll get some scissors. Oh, and I'll have to wash the *sakaki* buds."

"Here are some scissors." The Shirakawa woman held them out. "Your hearth is always so lovely. We flower vendors are certainly grateful for people like you."

"My mother is quite artistically sensitive."

"And you, too, Miss."

Chieko was silent.

"In so many homes now the hearths and the vases collect dust and the well covers are dirty. These days flower vendors are having a difficult time. It's too bad. But coming here to your house, I feel relieved and pleased."

Still Chieko did not speak. She could not bring herself to talk about how businesses that provide such personal service to homes seemed to be declining as the days passed.

Shige was still sitting at Takichiro's desk.

Chieko called her mother to the kitchen to show her what she had bought at the market. As Chieko removed items from the basket, her mother marveled at how frugal her daughter had become. Maybe it was because her father was away at the convent temple in Saga.

"I'll help," her mother said as she came into the kitchen. "Was that the flower woman who always comes?"

"Yes."

"Did your father have the book of paintings you gave him there with him at Saga?" her mother asked.

"I didn't notice it."

"He only took the ones he got from you, didn't he?"

The books contained paintings by Paul Klee, Matisse, Chagall, and also more modern abstract artists. Chieko had bought them for her father, thinking they might awaken in him a new sensitivity.

"It wouldn't matter if your father didn't draw any designs at all. It's enough just to handle goods that were dyed elsewhere. But your father . . . ," Shige said. "And you, Chieko, you're kind enough to wear only your father's kimonos. I should thank you," her mother continued.

"Thank me? I only wear them because I like them."

"Don't you think your father is sad when he sees the kimonos and obis his daughter wears?"

"Mother, they may seem plain, but if you look closely, they have a particular flavor. People compliment me on them."

Chieko recalled that she had had the same talk with her father earlier that day.

"Sometimes a pretty girl looks even prettier in a plain kimono, but . . . " Her mother lifted the lid from the pot and tested the boiling food with chopsticks. "I wonder why your father can't draw anything showy or fashionable anymore. He used to create quite striking and original designs."

"Don't you have any of Father's kimonos?"

"I'm too old to wear them now."

"Old? Old? How old are you?"

"On an old person . . ." Her mother stopped midsentence.

"What about the Intangible Cultural Treasures—living treasures, aren't they called? Komiya's Edo patterns. When young girls wear those they look even more striking. They stand out. People turn their heads when they pass."

"Your father could never be like Master Komiya."

"Father's designs come from the depth of a spiritual wave."

"You say such difficult things." Her mother's expression changed. Her skin was pure white, typical of a Kyoto woman. "But, Chieko, your father said he would make a dazzling kimono for your wedding. I've been looking forward to that for a long time."

"My wedding?" Chieko frowned and was silent for a while. "Mother, what's ever happened in your life that overturned your heart completely?"

"Maybe I've talked about this before, but the first time was when I got married and the other was when your father and I stole you away when you were a tiny baby. We picked you up and escaped by car. That was twenty years ago, but even now I feel a fluttering in my breast when I think of it. Chieko, please help calm your mother's heart."

"Mother, I was a foundling, an abandoned child, wasn't I?"

"No. No." Her mother shook her head rather sharply.

"Once or twice in their lives people do something frightfully evil," her mother continued. "Kidnapping a baby is a deeper sin than stealing money or anything else. Maybe it's more evil than murder. Your real parents were probably crazed with grief. When I think about it, even now I feel I want to return you, but it's too late. If you wanted to seek out your real parents, I couldn't stop you, but I would probably die."

"Mother, don't say such things. I have only one mother. I always felt that way as I was growing up."

"I understand. And that makes my sin all the worse. I realize that your father and I will go to hell. . . . What will hell be? Maybe it will be to have my dear child return to her original home."

Her mother's tone was severe, but tears were running down her cheeks. Chieko was holding back her own tears.

"Mother, please tell me the truth. I was a foundling, wasn't I?"

"No! I've told you that you weren't." Her mother shook her head again. "Why do you want to think you were a foundling?"

"I can't imagine that you and father would steal a child."

"Didn't I just tell you that once or twice in their lives, people do something fearfully evil that changes their hearts?"

"If it's true, where did you pick me up?"

"Under the cherry blossoms at night at Gion Shrine," her mother spoke without hesitation. "I may have told you before, but we sat down under the blossoms, and there was a lovely baby who'd been laid there to sleep. She looked up at me and smiled like a flower. I couldn't help but pick her up. When I did, my heart was pierced. I couldn't bear it. I pressed my cheek against hers. When I looked at your father's face he said, 'Shige, let's take this child.' 'What?' 'Hurry, let's go.' The rest is like a frantic dream. I think we jumped into the car in front of the soup shop at Hirano. The baby's mother had just stepped away for a moment. We stole her baby during that instant."

Her mother's story contained no implausible details.

"Fate . . . then you became our daughter. Twenty years have passed now. Whether it has been good for you or bad, I don't know. Even if it *has* been good for you, I'll always fold my hands and beg forgiveness in my heart. I think your father feels the same."

"It's been good, Mother. I think it has been good." Chieko put both her palms to her eyes.

Whether she was a foundling or whether she had been stolen, Chieko was registered as the legitimate daughter of the Sada family in the government records.

When she was first told by her parents that she was not really their daughter, Chieko could not believe it was true. Having just entered middle school, she doubted her parents' words, thinking they had told her the story because they were displeased with something about her.

Fearing she would hear something from the neighbors, her parents had decided to disclose the truth to her first, convinced that she loved them and that she had reached an age when she would understand.

Chieko was startled, but she was not so sad. It did not trouble her even when she reached adolescence. Her affection and love for Shige and Takichiro did not change. There was not so much as a hint of a problem that they might need to face. Such was Chieko's nature.

But if she was not really their daughter, then her true parents must be somewhere. And possibly she had brothers and sisters as well.

"I don't really want to see them, but . . . ," Chieko thought. "Certainly they have a more painful existence than I know here."

Chieko had no way of knowing. The poignancy of life with her father and mother, here in this old shop with its lattice doors and deep recesses, had moved Chieko to put her hands to her eyes in the kitchen.

"Chieko." Shige put her hands on her daughter's shoulders.

"Please don't ask about what happened long ago. Sometimes, in some places, there are gems that fall to this earth."

"A gem, a splendid gem. I wish it had been one you could have set in a ring." Chieko turned and began to work industriously.

After dinner Chieko and her mother cleaned up, then went upstairs to the back of the house.

The young shop boys slept in the low-ceilinged room with the lattice windows. The hall to the side of the center garden opened into the second floor. It could be reached from the shop as well. The Sadas had often entertained their favorite customers and put them up for the night in the second-story room. Now, they handled most business in the parlor facing the center garden. It was called a parlor, but it stretched from the shop to the back of the building. The dry goods and fabrics lay in stacks on either side and overflowed from the shelves. The room was long and wide, so it was a convenient place to unroll goods to display for their customers. A rattan mat was spread out on the floor all year long.

The ceiling was high in the rear of the second floor. There were two rooms that served as sleeping and living rooms for Chieko and her parents. Chieko sat at the mirror, undoing her long hair, which was always neatly arranged.

"Mother," Chieko called to the next room. Restless thoughts clouded her voice.

The Kimono Town

Although Kyoto is a large city, the color of the leaves there is beautiful.

The groves of pines in Gosho and the imperial villa of Shugakuin and the trees in the expansive gardens of the old temples all catch the eye of the traveler, as do the rows of weeping willows in the center of the city, along the banks of the Takase River. In Kiya, Gojo, and Horikawa, the willows truly weep, their branches drooping as if they would touch the ground. How gentle they are, these willows, and the red pines of Kitayama, whose branches sketch soft circles as they seem to join one to the next.

Now, it was spring in the old capital. The masses of young leaves formed patterns of color on the sides of Higashiyama and Hieizan.

The trees in Kyoto owed their striking appearance to the beauty and cleanliness of the town. In places like Gion, the narrow streets were never dirty where the small, somber, aging houses stood side by side.

In the area around Nishijin, as well, where the small dispirited kimono shops huddled together, the streets were clean. Dust never collected even on the fine latticework of the doors. In the Botanical Garden, too, not so much as a scrap of paper was to be found scattered about. The American military had built houses in the Botanical Garden, prohibiting, of course, any Japanese from entering, but now, with the occupation army gone, the gardens had been returned to their original state.

Otomo Sosuke, who lived in Nishijin, enjoyed the avenue lined with camphor trees in the Botanical Garden. The trees were not very tall, and the street was not long, but, before the occupation, he had often gone for a walk there when the leaves were sprouting. Sosuke sometimes wondered what had become of the trees, as he sat amid the clattering sound of the weaving looms. Surely the occupation army had not cut them down.

Sosuke had long awaited the reopening of the Botanical Garden. His customary walking path, from which he could see Kitayama, was just outside the garden, on the bank of the Kamo River.

Although the Botanical Garden was close to the Kamo River, it usually took Sosuke an hour to walk the distance. He had just been daydreaming of his walks when his wife called to him. "Mr. Sada is on the telephone. It seems he's in Saga."

"Takichiro? Calling from Saga?" Sosuke stepped to the counter.

Sosuke, the weaver, was four or five years younger than Sada, the wholesaler. Even outside their business dealings, they got along well. In their youth, there were times when they might have been called "bad company," but lately they had more or less drifted apart.

Sosuke answered the phone. "This is Otomo speaking. It's been a long time, hasn't it?"

"Ah, Otomo," Takichiro's voice reverberated.

"What are you doing at Saga?" Sosuke asked.

"I've secluded myself in a quiet convent temple."

"Please forgive me, but may I be so bold as to suggest that this is a rather dubious situation." Otomo spoke with mock politeness. "I've heard about those convents."

"No, this is a real convent temple. There's one old abbess and . . ."

"That's fine. Just one old abbess. For you, Sada, a young girl would be much too . . ."

"You fool," Takichiro laughed. "I have a favor to ask you today."

"Yes?"

"Would it be all right if I drop by shortly?"

"Certainly. Please do." Sosuke was suspicious. "I won't go anywhere. You can hear the looms over the phone, can't you?"

"Actually, that's what I want to talk to you about. It's good to hear that sound."

"What did you expect? What would I do if they stopped? This isn't some secluded convent."

It took less than half an hour for Sada Takichiro to reach Sosuke's shop by car. Sada's eyes seemed to shine as he quickly spread open his bundle.

"I wanted to ask you to weave this." He unrolled his design.

"Oh?" Sosuke stared into Takichiro's face. "This obi is rather up to date for you . . . showy. Hmm . . . Is this for some woman you're keeping in that convent temple?"

"Hardly." Takichiro laughed. "It's for my daughter."

"Really? I'm sure she'll be surprised when she sees it, but do you think she'd wear something like this?"

"The truth is Chieko herself gave me some books of Klee's paintings to inspire me."

"Klee? Who's Klee?"

"He is a painter who was in the forefront of the abstract movement. His paintings are gentle, exceptional. You might say they have the quality of a dream, a quality that would speak even to the heart of an old Japanese woman. I studied them over and over until I came up with this pattern. It's unlike any traditional Japanese design."

"Yes, it is."

"I was wondering how it would look as an obi, so I thought I'd have you weave it for me." Takichiro's pride would not be quelled.

Sosuke examined the design for a moment.

"Hmm, it's excellent. The color harmony . . . fine. You've never drawn anything so novel before; nevertheless, it's restrained. Weaving it will be difficult. But, we'll put our hearts into it and give it a try. The design shows your daughter's respect for her parents and her parents' affection for their daughter."

"Thank you. Nowadays, people would be quick to use an English word like 'idea' or 'sense.' Even colors are now referred to in faddish Western terms."

"Those aren't high-quality goods."

"I hate it that Western words have come into use. Haven't there been splendidly elegant colors in Japan since ancient times?"

"Even black has various subtle shades," Sosuke nodded. "Yes, I was just thinking about that today. There are some obi makers like Izukura. They have a modern factory in a four-story Western-style building. Nishijin will probably go the same way. They make five hundred obis a day and soon the employees will be taking part in the company's management. The average age of the employees is in the twenties and thirties. Small home businesses like mine with hand looms will probably disappear within twenty or thirty years."

"That's ridiculous."

"If one survived, wouldn't it have to be under government sponsorship as an 'Intangible Cultural Treasure'? . . . Why, even a person like you, Sada, with your Klee or whatever . . ."

"I *did* mention Paul Klee, but that's not all. I secluded myself in that convent for ten days—no, two weeks—racking my brain day and night. Aren't the colors and pattern sophisticated?" Takichiro asked.

"Very sophisticated and refined. Elegant in a Japanese manner," Sosuke hurriedly continued. "I recognize that it is indeed your work. We'll weave it into a fine obi for you. I'll send the design to a good shop to have the weaving pattern for the loom cards drafted accurately. I think I'll have Hideo weave it rather than myself. He's my eldest son. You know him, don't you?"

"Yes."

"His weaving is much more precise than my own," Sosuke said.

"Well, I leave it to your judgment. I call myself a kimono wholesaler, but all I ever do is ship goods out to the little country places."

"Don't say such things."

"Anyway, I know this isn't a summer obi. It *is* for autumn, but I'd like to see it as soon as possible."

"I see. What about a kimono to go with it?"

"I've only thought about the obi so far."

"Since you're a wholesale dealer, I suppose you can pick out anything you like from your stock, so it doesn't matter which you choose first. Are you doing this in preparation for your daughter's marriage?"

"No. No." Takichiro began to blush as if the question were about himself.

The craft of hand weaving is said to be a difficult skill to pass down for three generations. Even if the father were a superior weaver, even if he had, so to speak, an artist's hand, his ability would not necessarily be inherited by his children. It is not that a son would purposely neglect his work, resting on his father's accomplishments, but the son might turn out to be untalented although he may strive earnestly.

Often a child is first taught to reel thread when he is four or five. Then, at ten or twelve, he receives training as an apprentice weaver. Finally, he is able to weave for wages. For that reason, having a large number of children often helps a family to prosper. Even an old woman of sixty or seventy can reel silk inside the house, so, in many homes, a grandmother and her little granddaughter sit working together.

In Otomo Sosuke's house, his old wife wound the obi thread. Sitting day in and day out working with eyes downcast had aged her beyond her years and made her silent.

Otomo had three sons, each of whom wove obis at his own loom. Owning three looms was, of course, better than average; many shops had only one, while others had to rent their looms. Hideo's skill had surpassed his father's and was known even among the wholesale dealers and other weavers.

"Hideo, Hideo," Sosuke called, but his son seemed not to hear. Unlike the countless machine looms of the large factories, the three wooden looms in Sosuke's shop did not make much noise. Sosuke thought he had called quite loudly enough, but his voice did not seem to reach Hideo, who was sitting at the loom farthest away, near the garden, absorbed in weaving a difficult lined obi.

"Mother, would you tell Hideo to come here," Sosuke said to his wife.

"Yes." She brushed her lap and stepped down into the entry room. As she walked toward Hideo's loom, she beat the small of her back with her fists to relax the strain of sitting so long.

Stopping the reed batten of the loom, Hideo glanced toward his father, but he did not stand up immediately. Possibly he was tired, but, knowing that a customer was watching, he could not flex his arms or stretch his back. Finally, he mopped his face and approached his father and Takichiro.

"Thank you for coming. I'm sorry the place is such a mess," he greeted Takichiro sullenly. His work seemed to linger in his face and body.

"Mr. Sada has designed an obi, and we're going to weave it for him," his father said.

"I see." Hideo's voice displayed no enthusiasm.

"This is an important obi, so rather than putting my hand to it, I think it would be better to have you weave it."

"Is it for your daughter, Chieko?" Hideo turned his ashen face toward Sada for the first time.

Hideo's expression was rather inhospitable for a man of Kyoto. His father, Sosuke, tried to make excuses for him.

"Hideo's tired from working all morning."

"It's wonderful that he can be so absorbed in his work." Takichiro tried to console him.

"It's just a lined obi, but I was completely engrossed in it. Forgive me." Hideo bowed his head.

"That's all right. A weaver must be that way." Takichiro nodded twice.

"Even some trivial item will be recognized as the work of our shop, so it is distressing always having to be so cautious." Hideo looked down.

"Hideo," Sosuke put new resolve in his voice. "Mr. Sada's design is different. He secluded himself in a convent in Saga to draw it. It won't be for sale."

"Really. Hmm . . . a convent in Saga . . ."

"Have him show it to you."

Takichiro had come to Otomo's shop in high spirits, but they were dampened considerably by Hideo's attitude.

He unrolled the drawing in front of the silent Hideo. "What do you think?" Takichiro asked timidly.

Hideo stared without speaking.

"Isn't it any good?"

Still Hideo did not answer.

Sosuke lost patience with his son's stubborn silence. "Hideo, don't you think it's rude not to respond?"

"Yes." He still did not look up. "I'm a weaver, so I'm examining Mr. Sada's design. This isn't some insignificant piece. This obi is for Chieko, isn't it?"

"Yes, it is," his father nodded. He was suspicious of Hideo's abnormal manner.

"It isn't any good, is it?" Takichiro repeated, his tone becoming more severe.

"It's fine," Hideo was calm. "I never said it wasn't good."

"You didn't say it, but in your heart . . . those eyes said so."

"Really?"

"What do you mean . . ." Takichiro stood and struck Hideo in the face. Hideo did not try to dodge the blow.

"Hit me as much as you'd like. I would never dream of telling you your design was poor." Possibly because of the blow, Hideo's face became animated.

Hideo bowed low and apologized, not bothering to nurse his reddening cheek.

"Mr. Sada, forgive me."

Takichiro did not speak, so Hideo went on, "You may be offended, but I want to weave this obi."

"That's what I came for . . . to ask you." Takichiro tried to calm his chest. "Please forgive me. I'm older and should know better. . . . My hand hurts from hitting you."

"I should have lent you my hand. The skin of a weaver's hand is tough."

The two of them laughed, but the distress deep within Takichiro's heart would not fade.

"How many years has it been since I hit someone? So many, I can't recall. Well, I've already asked you to forgive me for that. What I want to ask you is this, Hideo. When you looked at my design, why did you make such a queer face? Would you tell me truthfully?"

"Yes." Hideo frowned again. "I'm young and just a laborer, so I don't understand such things well. But you said you secluded yourself in a convent in Saga to draw the design, didn't you?"

"Yes, I was at the temple today. Let's see. It's been about two weeks since . . ."

"Give it up!" Hideo spoke forcefully. "Go back home."

"I can't relax at home."

"This obi design is bright, showy, innovative, but I found

it somehow alarming. I wondered how you could have drawn a design like this. That's why I was staring at it. . . . It's intriguing at first glance, but it has none of the harmony of a warm heart. It's raging and morbid."

Takichiro turned pale, his lips trembling. Words would not come.

"There are probably foxes and badgers around that desolate temple. I don't mean to say that you've been bewitched by them, but . . ."

Takichiro pulled the design toward his knees and stared at it intently. "Well, thank you for what you've said. You're an impressive fellow for a young man. Thank you. I'll think about this once more and draw it over again." Takichiro hurriedly rolled up the design and stuffed it into his pocket.

"Don't! It's fine as it is. When it's woven, it will have a different feeling about it. The fabric and dyed threads will make the color . . ."

"Thank you, Hideo. Would you weave it after I warm the color with the affection I have for my daughter?" Takichiro excused himself, going out through the gate.

Just outside, there was a small stream that seemed befitting of the capital. Old grass grew along the bank, leaning in toward the water. The white wall by the bank was probably part of Otomo's house.

Takichiro crumpled the obi design in his pocket. Then taking it out, he tossed it into the stream.

Shige was puzzled by Takichiro's unexpected phone call from Saga asking if she would come to Omuro with Chieko to see the flowers. Shige had never gone out flower viewing with her husband.

"Chieko, Chieko," Shige called to her daughter as if requesting help. "It's your father. Will you take it?"

Chieko took the phone, listening with her hand on her mother's shoulder.

"Yes, I'll bring Mother, too. Wait for us at the tearoom in front of Ninnaji Temple. Yes . . . as soon as we can."

Chieko hung up the telephone. Smiling, she spoke to her mother. "It's an invitation to go flower viewing. I'm surprised he's invited you, too."

"Why would he ask me?"

"He says the cherry blossoms at Omuro are at their best now."

Chieko hurried her hesitant mother along as they left the shop. Shige still looked suspicious.

The dawn cherries and the double cherries at Omuro were blooming later than most in the town, possibly the last traces of cherry blossoms still left in the capital.

The grove of cherries inside the main gate to the left of Ninnaji was overflowing with blossoms.

Large benches were lined up along a path in the cherry grove, and there was a great commotion of people drinking and singing in a boisterous crowd. Some old country women were dancing gaily, while the drunken men lay asleep, snoring. Some of the men even rolled off the benches.

"I can't stand it. This is terrible." Takichiro stood up, lamenting the scene. The three of them did not go in among the blossoms. Takichiro had known the cherries of Omuro long ago.

Smoke rose among the trees in the rear of the garden from fires where trash left by the sightseers was being burned.

"Let's go some place quiet. Shall we, Shige?" Takichiro asked.

As they turned to go, they saw near some benches six or seven Korean girls in Korean dress beating Korean drums and dancing a Korean dance under the tall pines across from the cherry grove. This would certainly be a far more elegant sight. One could glimpse the mountain cherries among the pines.

Chieko paused to watch the Korean dance.

"Father, a quiet place would be better. How about the Botanical Garden?"

"That might be all right. All you need to do is take just one look at the cherries at Omuro, and you've done your duty to spring." Takichiro went out the main gate and got into the car.

The Botanical Garden had just reopened in April. The train from Kyoto station to the garden had begun to run more frequently.

"If there are crowds at the Botanical Garden, let's take a walk by the Kamo River instead," Takichiro said to Shige.

The automobile passed through the green of the town. The new leaves stood out more vividly against the background of old homes imbued with antique colors than they did against the new houses.

The Botanical Garden opened up wide beyond the gate in front of the tree-lined avenue. The bank of the Kamo River was to the left.

Shige slipped the entrance passes into her obi. Her heart opened as she gazed at the expansive scenery. Only the tops of the mountains were visible from the kimono town, and Shige seldom even went out to the street in front of the shop.

Tulips were blooming around the fountain in the front of the Botanical Garden.

"This isn't something you would normally see in Kyoto," Shige said. "It's no wonder the Americans made their homes here."

"I think they were built farther toward the back," Takichiro said.

As they approached the fountain, a fine spray was scattered in the air, though there was not much of a breeze. A large, round, steel-frame greenhouse stood on the far left side of the fountain. The three of them glanced at the tropical plants inside, but did not enter, since they had only a short time to walk.

A huge Himalayan pine to the right of the path was putting forth new shoots. The lower branches of the tree spread out just above the ground. Although it is called a "needle tree," the soft green of the new buds did not suggest needles; instead, they had a dreamlike air.

"Otomo and his son certainly got the best of me," Takichiro said out of the blue. "I've sent them a lot of work. Their eyes are sharp; they can see right to the heart." Shige and Chieko naturally did not quite understand Takichiro's monologue.

"Did you see Hideo?" Chieko asked.

"I hear he's a good weaver," Shige said. Takichiro usually did not like to be pressed for details.

They went around the right side of the fountain. At the end of the walkway was a children's playground. Many voices could be heard, and the children's satchels were arranged together on the ground.

As the Sadas turned to the right in the shadow of the trees, the path unexpectedly descended toward a tulip field. The flowers in full bloom were so exquisite that Chieko almost spoke out loud. Red, yellow, white, and purple as dark as a black camellia, each blooming in its own field.

"Seeing this makes me think I should use tulips in a kimono pattern. I had thought it would be ridiculous," Takichiro sighed.

As he continued to look at the fields, Takichiro wondered to himself—if the low branches of the budding Himalayan cedar are said to resemble a peacock spreading its tail feathers, to what could one compare the multicolored tulips blooming so profusely here?

These colors seemed to tint the sky and reflect within one's own body.

Shige moved away from her husband slightly, drawing up next to her daughter. Chieko thought it strange, but her face did not show it.

"Mother, that group of people in front of the white tulip field looks like a *miai*," Chieko whispered as she glanced at a young couple whose first arranged meeting was taking place in front of the flowers.

"Yes, it does."

"Don't stare at them, Mother." Chieko pulled her sleeve.

A pond with carp in it lay in front of the tulip fields.

Takichiro stood up from the bench and walked over to see the tulips up close. He stooped down, peering into the mass of flowers. Then he returned to Chieko and his wife.

"Western flowers are bright, but I tire of them. Of course, I like a bamboo grove best."

Shige and Chieko stood up.

The tulip fields were in a hollow surrounded by trees.

"Chieko, the Botanical Garden is designed after Western-style gardens, isn't it?" Takichiro asked his daughter.

"I'm not certain, but I think it is, partly," Chieko answered. "Could we stay a bit longer, for Mother?"

Takichiro walked off among the flowers as if he had better things to do.

"Mr. Sada?" A voice called. "It is! Mr. Sada!"

"Ah, Mr. Otomo, and Hideo, too," Takichiro said. "What a surprise."

"I'm the one who's surprised." Sosuke bowed deeply. "I like the camphor tree avenue, so I've been waiting for the garden to reopen. The trees are fifty or sixty years old, and I always used to take leisurely walks among them." Sosuke bowed his head again. "I'm sorry my son was so rude to you the other day."

"He's young."

"Did you come here from Saga?"

"Yes, I did, but Chieko and Shige came from home and met me here."

Sosuke stepped over to greet Chieko and Shige.

"Hideo, what do you think of these tulips?" Takichiro asked rather sternly.

"Flowers are living." Hideo's manner was still brusque.

"Living? That's for certain. But I've grown tired of them . . . such an awful lot of flowers."

"Flowers are living. Their life is short, but they live conspicuously. In the coming year they will bud and bloom . . . just as nature lives."

Takichiro felt once again that Hideo had cut him.

"My eye just isn't accustomed to them. I wouldn't like an obi or kimono cloth in a tulip pattern, but if a great artist were to create such a painting, even tulips could become a work with an eternal life," Takichiro said, looking aside. "Some of the ancient designs were like that. Some of them are older than this capital city itself. No one can create anything like that anymore. They can do no more than copy them. . . . Aren't there even trees here, still living, that are older than the capital?"

"I didn't mean anything as difficult as that. A weaver who hears the clatter of the wooden looms every day doesn't think such lofty thoughts." Hideo lowered his head. "But this is an example. Were your daughter to stand before the statue of Miroku at Koryuji Temple or Chuguji Temple, how much more beautiful would she be in comparison."

"Would you tell that to Chieko? That would make her happy. It's a shame to waste such thoughts on me."

"That's why I said the tulips were living." Power entered Hideo's voice. "They flower for only a short season, but don't they bloom with all their strength? Now is their time."

"That's true." Takichiro turned back toward Hideo.

"I don't think of myself as weaving obis that will be worn and passed down for generations. As for now, I'm weaving obis that a girl can be happy wearing for even a year."

"That's a good attitude."

"I have to be that way. I'm not like Tatsumura."

Takichiro did not speak.

"That's the feeling that prompted me to say that the tulips were alive. Now is their prime, but there are already a few fallen petals."

"Yes, there are."

"Even fallen petals . . . well, a blizzard of cherry blossoms has an elegance about it, but what about tulips?"

"Do you mean the sight of tulip petals scattered about?" Takichiro asked. "I feel rather repulsed by such masses of flowers. The colors are too gaudy and they seem to have no 'flavor.' Of course, I'm older."

"Let's go," Hideo urged Takichiro. "I've seen tulip patterns for obis before, but the ones that come to our shop are not of living flowers. My eyes have been opened."

The five of them climbed the stone steps from the tulip fields in the hollow. To the side of the steps, the masses of Kirishima azalea bushes swelled upward more like a living embankment than a hedge. They were not in flower now, but the abundance of delicate, young, green leaves set off the colors of the blooming tulips to their best advantage.

At the top of the steps were two new, unfamiliar peony gardens, not yet in flower.

Hieizan was visible to the east.

One could see Hieizan, Kitayama, and Higashiyama from almost anywhere in the Botanical Garden, but Hieizan in the east looked as if it marked the main entrance to the peony garden.

"Perhaps it's because of the deep haze, but doesn't Hieizan appear low?" Sosuke asked Takichiro.

"It's a spring mist . . . gentle . . . " Takichiro gazed at it for a moment. "Yes, it is, but doesn't this heavy mist make you think of the fleeting spring?"

"Yes."

"Such a deep haze makes me realize that spring will soon come to an end."

"Yes," Sosuke said again. "It passes so quickly. I seldom go flower viewing anymore."

"There's nothing new to see."

The two of them walked quietly for a moment.

"Otomo, before we go, let's walk through the camphor tree avenue you said you liked," Takichiro said.

"Thank you. Let's do. It's enough for me just to walk among those trees. I passed by them on the way in." Sosuke turned back to Chieko. "Chieko, come walk up here with us."

The ends of the branches of the camphor trees on either side mingled in the center above the avenue. The new leaves on the branch tips were still supple and a faint red in color. There was little wind, but here and there the branches rustled slightly. The five of them spoke little, but within each, their thoughts were churning in the shade of the trees.

Having heard Hideo compare Chieko to the most graceful Buddhist statues of Nara and Kyoto, saying Chieko was more beautiful, Takichiro could not get those words out of his mind. Could Hideo be so attracted to Chieko?

If Chieko were to marry Hideo, they would need her in Sosuke's weaving shop. Would she reel silk from morning until night just like Hideo's mother?

When Takichiro looked back, he saw that Chieko was absorbed in a conversation with Hideo. Occasionally, she nodded.

Marriage would not necessarily mean she would have to go to Otomo's house. Takichiro thought it might be possible to bring Hideo into his own home as an adopted son-in-law.

Chieko was an only child. Were she to leave home, how lonely her mother, Shige, would be.

But Hideo was himself the eldest son, and Otomo had said that Hideo was a more accomplished weaver than his father. Even so, there were also two younger sons.

Besides, Takichiro's business had declined so much he could not even afford to remodel the inside of the old-style shop. But he was, after all, a wholesaler of dry goods in the old neighborhood of Nakagyo, and not a weaver. Otomo's shop was known as a family handicraft business without a single outside employee. The nature of the shop manifested itself in the appearance of Hideo's mother, Asako, and in their humble kitchen. Though Hideo was the eldest boy, Otomo's manner seemed to indicate he might offer his son to be taken into the Sada home as Chieko's husband.

"Hideo is a fine, dependable fellow," Takichiro said, testing Sosuke's response. "He's young, but he's certainly reliable."

"Thank you," Sosuke said casually. "Only as far as his trade goes. He works hard, but he's rude with people. He's quite unstable."

"There's nothing wrong with that. I'm that way myself. He scolded me quite thoroughly. . . ." Takichiro's manner was pleasant.

"I'm sorry he acted the way he did." Sosuke lowered his head slightly. "He doesn't listen to anything we say unless he already agrees."

"That's all right." Takichiro nodded. "Why did you bring only Hideo with you today?"

"If I were to bring his brothers, too, the looms would have to stop. Besides, he's so strong headed, I thought a walk among the camphor trees would calm him a bit."

"This is a lovely avenue. Actually, Otomo, I brought Shige and Chieko here to the Botanical Garden because of Hideo's . . . well, his advice."

"What?" Sosuke glared dubiously at Takichiro's face. "You wanted to see your daughter's face, didn't you?"

"No. No." Takichiro hurriedly denied it.

Sosuke looked around. Chieko and Hideo were walking several paces back. Shige was alone even farther behind.

As they went out the gate of the Botanical Garden, Takichiro spoke to Sosuke, "Please take our car. Nishijin is close. Meanwhile, we'll walk along the banks of the river."

Sosuke hesitated, but Hideo urged his father into the car first, saying, "Let's accept Mr. Sada's hospitality."

As Sada stood seeing them off, Sosuke sat up on the seat to bow, but Hideo's movement was so slight one could not distinguish whether or not he had nodded his head.

"He's an interesting boy." Takichiro recalled the time he had hit Hideo in the face. Suppressing a smile, he said to his daughter, "You and Hideo certainly had a long talk. Is he shy with girls?"

Chieko's eyes looked sheepish. "On the camphor tree avenue? All I did was listen. I wondered why he talked to me so much. Why should he open up to someone like me?"

"Isn't it because he likes you? You understand that much, don't you? He said you were more beautiful than the Miroku at Chuguji or Koryuji Temple. I was surprised, too. That obstinate fellow says some amazing things."

Startled, Chieko did not speak. She blushed lightly to the base of her neck.

"What did you talk about?" her father asked.

"About the fate of the hand weavers at Nishijin."

"Fate?" Her father seemed to become absorbed in thought.

" 'Fate' makes it sound like some difficult conversation, but, yes, we talked about their fate," Chieko answered.

Outside the Botanical Garden were pine trees growing in a row on an embankment of the Kamo River. Takichiro stepped down through the trees to the river bottom. The bed of the Kamo was like a long narrow field of young grass. The sound of water falling over a dam suddenly became audible.

A group of old people sat in the grass with their picnic lunch spread out around them. Young men and women were walking together.

On the far bank was a promenade just below the road. Beyond the cherry trees with their scattering of new leaves was Atagoyama in the center and Nishiyama stretching to either side behind. Upstream, Kitayama seemed to be very near.

"Shall we sit down here?" Shige asked. Beyond Kitaoji Bridge one could glimpse Yuzen silk spread out to dry on the river plain.

"It's a lovely spring," Takichiro said to his wife, who was gazing about. "Shige, what do you think of that boy, Hideo?"

"What do you mean, 'what do I think'?"

"What if we brought him into our home to marry Chieko?"

"What? Why should you bring up something like that so suddenly?"

"He's a fine boy, isn't he?"

"Yes, but you'll have to ask Chieko about such things."

"Chieko has always said she'd be completely obedient." Takichiro looked at his daughter. "Haven't you, Chieko?"

"You can't force your opinion on someone in a question like marriage." Shige also turned toward Chieko.

Chieko cast her eyes down. A vision of Mizuki Shin'ichi came to mind. It was Shin'ichi as a child, a festival boy with finely drawn eyebrows, lip rouge, and makeup, wearing ancient imperial clothing and riding on a float at the Gion Festival. Of course, at that time, Chieko, too, had been but a child.

Kitayama Cedars

Since the days of the Heian Court, the most noted mountain of Kyoto was Hieizan, and the most noted festival was the Kamo Festival.

The Hollyhock Festival of May fifteenth had already passed.

Since 1956 the Procession of Imperial Messengers of the Hollyhock Festival had been combined with the Procession of Shrine Maidens. The participants would perform the old ritual of purifying themselves in the Kamo River before shutting themselves up in the purification hall. Reviving the ancient practices, court women wearing elegant robes led the procession in a palanquin, followed by ladies in waiting and maidens of the court, with court minstrels who offered music. The shrine maidens rode in traditional oxcarts.

One of Chieko's schoolmates had been chosen to be a shrine maiden. Chieko and her friends had gone to the banks of the Kamo to see their companion in the procession. The shrine maidens looked gay in their elegant clothing, more because they were usually college-age girls than because of their dress.

It almost seemed that there was a large or small festival every day in Kyoto. Looking at a festival calendar, one would think there was always something going on in May. It would be impossible to attend all the tea offerings, imperial excursions, and tea ceremonies.

This May, Chieko had missed even the Hollyhock Festival, partly because of the heavy rains, and partly because she had always had someone to take her to all the festivals since she was a little girl.

Besides flowers, Chieko also enjoyed going to view the green of the young leaves. She was naturally fond of the newly budding maples at Takaoji and Wakaoji.

As she put on some tea someone had sent from Uji, Chieko said, "Mother, I forgot to go see the gathering of the new tea this year."

"They're still picking the tea leaves now, aren't they?" her mother asked.

"Possibly."

They had also been a bit late, too, to see the flowerlike beauty of the opening buds of the camphor trees through which they had walked at the Botanical Gardens.

Chieko received a telephone call from her friend Masako.

"Chieko, would you like to go to Takao to see the new maple leaves?" she asked. "There aren't as many people as when the leaves turn in the autumn."

"Isn't it late for them?"

"It's cooler there than in town. I think they're still all right."

"Hmm," Chieko cut her off shortly. "Say, after the cherries at Heian Shrine, it would have been pleasant to have seen the ones in the mountains, but I completely forgot about them. I wonder about that one old tree. . . . The cherry blossoms are gone, but I would like to see the cedars at Kitayama. That's near Takao, isn't it? Whenever I see the lovely straight cedars at Kitayama, my spirit feels refreshed. Could we go as far as Kitayama? I'd rather see the cedars than the maples."

Having come so far, Chieko and Masako decided to see the young maple leaves at Jingoji Temple in Takao, Saimyoji Temple at Makinoo, and Kozanji Temple at Toganoo before they went on. Both Jingoji Temple and Kozanji Temple were at the top of a steep slope.

Masako could climb easily, dressed in low heels and light

Western clothes suitable for early summer, but she looked back wondering how Chieko was doing dressed in a kimono. Chieko spoke without a trace of difficulty. "Why are you looking at me that way?"

"How beautiful."

"Yes, it is beautiful." Chieko stood still, looking down on the Kiyotaki River. "I thought the green would be more vivid, but it is cool, isn't it?"

"I . . ." Masako tried to stifle a smile. "Chieko, I was talking about you."

Chieko did not speak.

"Why was such a beautiful girl born?"

"Oh, stop it."

"Your plain kimono makes you look all the more lovely here amid the green of the trees. A bright kimono would be quite showy, but . . ."

Chieko was wearing a rather somber violet kimono, and her obi was made from the chintz her father had cut so ungrudgingly. She had heard Masako say the same thing many times before.

Chieko climbed the stone steps. At the moment Masako spoke, Chieko had been thinking of the faint reddish traces on a painting she had seen. Had it been on the portrait of Shigemori, or elsewhere? The portraits of Taira no Shigemori and Minamoto no Yorimasa in Jingoji Temple had been made world famous by André Malraux.

At Kozanji Temple Chieko enjoyed viewing the mountains from the veranda of the Sekisuiin. She was also fond of the portrait that hung there of the founder of the sect of the temple, the priest Myoe, sitting in a tree meditating. A reproduction of the Chojugiga scroll lay unrolled to the side of the alcove. The two girls were served tea on the veranda.

Masako had never gone farther than Kozanji Temple. Most sightseers stopped there.

Chieko recalled the times when her father had taken her around the mountains to see the cherry blossoms. They gathered long thick horsetail grasses to take home. Since she had come as far as Takao, Chieko decided to go to the Kitayama cedar village even if she had to go alone. Actually, the village had merged with the city and was properly called Nakagawa Kitayama District of Kita Ward, but there were only two or three hundred houses, so "village" seemed a more appropriate term.

"I'm accustomed to walking, so I'll go on foot," Chieko said. "Besides, this is such a good road."

The steep mountains lined the banks of the Kiyotaki River where they walked. Finally, the beautiful cedar groves came into view. The straight cedar trees revealed the thoughtful attention given them. This village was the only place that produced the renowned Kitayama logs.

Some women who had been cutting grass came down the hill from among the cedars for a three o'clock break.

Masako stood frozen, staring at one of the girls. "Chieko, that girl resembles you quite a bit. She looks just like you, don't you think?"

The girl had rolled up the tube sleeves of her navy blue kimono. She was wearing loose trousers and an apron with old-style gloves on her hands and a hand towel draped over her head the way working women always wore them. The apron was wrapped all the way around to the back, and her kimono had openings under the arms. A glimpse of her narrow red obi showed between her sleeves and her trousers. The other women were dressed in a similar fashion. They resembled the Ohara women; however, unlike the Ohara peddler women, their clothing was not a costume to wear when selling things in the city, but real mountain work clothes.

"She really does look like you. Don't you think it's strange?" Masako looked at the girl closely.

"What?" Chieko gave a cursory glance. "You're always so rash."

"It doesn't matter how rash I am. You don't see someone as beautiful as she is . . ."

"She is beautiful, but . . ."

"It's as if she were your own lost child."

"See how excited you get?"

Masako started to laugh at her own remark, but hearing Chieko's words she kept silent for a moment.

"I know it's possible for one person to resemble another that much, but this is frightening, Masako said."

The girl and those with her passed by, paying little attention to Chieko and Masako.

The towel on the girl's head revealed a glimpse of her hair in front, but half hid her face. She was not looking toward Chieko and Masako, so they could not distinguish her features. Chieko had visited the mountain village several times and seen the men strip the rough bark from the cedar logs after which the women would remove the remaining traces, polishing the logs with sand mixed with warm water. She thought she vaguely recognized all the girls' faces, since they did their work on the roadside, outdoors in the open air. There were probably few young girls in such a small mountain village, but Chieko, of course, had not inspected each of the girls' faces carefully.

Masako calmed down as she watched the women walking away.

"How strange," she said. Then she tilted her head, gazing at Chieko as if she had not looked at her before.

"She *does* look like you."

"In what way?" Chieko asked.

"Well, it's her overall appearance. It's hard to say just how she resembles you. Her nose . . . or eyes . . . of course, you would expect a girl from the city and a girl from the mountains to be quite different. Please forgive me."

"That's all right."

"Chieko, couldn't we follow that girl home and have another look?" Masako asked, reluctant to drop the subject.

Even someone as venturesome as Masako was probably not serious when she suggested they follow the girl.

Chieko slowed her pace almost to a halt, looking up at the beautiful polished cedar logs of uniform diameter that stood leaning in rows against the houses.

"They look like handicraft items," Chieko said. "I hear they use them in the construction of rooms for the tea ceremony as far away as Tokyo and Kyushu."

The logs stood in a line against the eaves of a house and along the second floor as well. Underwear was hanging out to dry in front of the rows on the second story. Masako looked at the house, amazed. "These people live inside a parade of cedars," she said.

"You get in such a hurry, Masako," Chieko laughed. "Look, there. Isn't that a splendid house next to the shed with the logs?"

"Oh, I saw the laundry hanging out to dry there, so I thought that building was the house."

"The same rash thinking made you say that girl looked like me."

"That was different." Masako became serious. "Were you really so upset when I said she resembled you?"

"No, not in the least." Just as Chieko spoke, the girl's eyes came unexpectedly to mind. A rich, deep poignancy lay submerged in the vision of the eyes of that healthy, hardworking girl.

"The women in this village do work awfully hard," Chieko said, seemingly to escape from Masako's conversation.

"It is nothing unusual for a woman to labor right alongside a man. Farmers are like that, aren't they? Greengrocers and shopkeepers, too," Masako said casually. "A genteel girl like you *would* be impressed by such things."

"I work. You must be talking about yourself."

"That's right. I don't work," Masako said frankly.

"It's easy to talk about labor, but I wanted to show you how these village women really work." Chieko again looked up at the cedar mountains. "They've already started the branch cutting."

"What do you mean, 'branch cutting'?"

"They cut off unnecessary branches with a hatchet to produce good trees for logs. Sometimes they use ladders, but often they have to jump from tree to tree like monkeys."

"How dangerous!"

"I hear some men climb up in the morning and don't come down until lunchtime."

Masako, too, looked up at the cedar mountains. The straight trunks were beautiful standing so orderly. The clusters of leaves left on the branches resembled a fine crafted work.

The mountains were neither high nor deep. The trunk of each individual tree was visible even on the tops of the mountains. The cedars were used in the construction of tearooms so the appearance of the groves themselves had the elegant air of the tea ceremony.

The mountains on either side of Kiyotaki River were steep, their sides dropping down into the narrow valley. One reason the famous cedar logs were raised here was that the area received ample rain and little sunshine. It was also protected from the wind. Were a strong wind to strike the trees, the softness of the new growth ring would allow them to grow bent or twisted.

The houses of the village stood in a single row along the riverbank at the foot of the mountain.

Chieko and Masako walked to the far side beyond the village, then returned.

They saw a house where logs were being polished. The women lifted the logs from the water where they had been soaking and polished them carefully with Bodai sand. The sand, which resembled reddish-yellow clay, was brought from beneath Bodai Falls.

"What will happen when the sand runs out?" Masako asked.

"The water brings sand with it when it rains, and it collects at the bottom of the falls," an elderly woman answered.

Masako thought this was a pleasant conversation.

As Chieko had explained, the women were working diligently with their hands. The log they were polishing was about five or six inches in diameter; it would probably be used for a pillar.

The women washed the polished logs in water and set them aside to dry. Then they wrapped them in paper or straw to be shipped off.

Cedars were planted all the way down the slopes of the mountain to the riverbed of Kiyotaki River. The arrangement of the cedars standing on the mountains and those leaning in rows against the eaves of the houses reminded Masako of the Bengara lattice doors in the houses of old Kyoto.

The Bodai Road stop of the Japan National Railway Bus Line was located at the entrance to the village, just down from the falls. There the two girls boarded the bus for home. After a silence, Masako suddenly spoke, "I wonder if it's best for a girl to grow up straight like those cedars."

Chieko did not speak.

"But we don't receive as affectionate care as the trees."

Chieko almost burst out laughing. "Masako, are you seeing someone?"

"Yes, I am. We often sit together in the grass on the bank of the Kamo River. Recently, there have been more visitors coming to the river plain at Kiyamachi, so now they turn the lights on at night. But we always sit facing the rear so no one will recognize us."

"What about tonight?"

"Tonight we have a date at seven-thirty, though it is still a little bit light then."

Chieko envied Masako's freedom.

Chieko and her parents sat at dinner in the back parlor facing the inner garden.

"Today the Shimamuras sent us some Hyomasa bamboo leaf sushi. I'm sorry. All I made for dinner was some soup to go with it," Shige said to Takichiro.

Bamboo leaf sushi made with sea bream was Takichiro's favorite dish.

"The sushi was a bit late being delivered," Shige said. Then she spoke of her daughter. "Chieko went to see the Kitayama cedars again with Masako."

The sushi was piled on an Imari porcelain dish. Inside each of the triangularly folded bamboo leaves, a thin slice of sea bream rested on top of the rice. The soup contained mostly dried tofu and some mushrooms.

Takichiro's business still retained the air of an old Kyoto shop, exemplified by the Bengara lattice door, but now that his business was incorporated, most of the clerks and shop boys had started commuting to work as regular company employees. With only two or three live-in shop boys from Omi in the lattice window room in the front of the second floor, the rear of the house was quiet at dinnertime.

"You like going to the Kitayama cedar village, don't you?" her mother said. "Why is that?"

"The cedars all stand there so straight and beautiful. I wish human hearts grew like that."

"Then aren't you just like them?" her mother asked.

"No, I'm bent and twisted. . . ."

"That's true," her father spoke up. "No matter how gentle a person may be, deep inside he still has much to ponder . . . but isn't that all right? A child like the Kitayama cedars would be sweet, but no such child exists. And were there such a child, someday he would probably meet with suffering. I think, as long as a tree grows tall, it doesn't matter if it's bent or twisted. Take a look at the old maple in our small garden."

"What do you mean saying such things to a good child like Chieko?" Her mother grew angry.

"I know. I know. Chieko is straight and . . ."

Chieko turned her face toward the inner garden and was silent for a moment.

"I don't have the kind of strength that maple has." Chieko's voice was touched with sadness. "I am closer to the violets growing in the hollows of the tree. . . . Oh, I hadn't noticed until now. The violet flowers are gone."

"They are, but they'll surely bloom again next spring," her mother said.

Chieko's gaze rested on the Christian lantern at the base of the maple. She could not see the weatherworn carving very well in the dim light from the house, but somehow she wanted to pray.

"Mother, where was I really born?"

Shige looked at Takichiro.

"Under the evening cherry blossoms of Gion," her father said flatly.

Hearing her father say she was born under the cherry trees at Gion reminded her of the children's story, "The Tale of the Bamboo Cutter," in which the tiny princess Kaguyahime was found between the joints of a stalk of bamboo.

That is why he had spoken very matter-of-factly.

If it were true that she had been born under the flowers, maybe someone would come from the moon to meet her, as in the story of Kaguyahime. Chieko realized the humor of her father's explanation, but she could not bring herself to mention it out loud.

Whether she had been a foundling or a stolen child, her mother and father would not know where she was born, nor would they know who her real parents were.

Chieko regretted that she had asked amiss, but it seemed best not to apologize. What had prompted her to inquire so unexpectedly? She did not quite understand, but perhaps she vaguely recalled Masako telling her that she looked just like the girl at the Kitayama cedar village.

Chieko did not know where to avert her eyes. She gazed at the top of the large maple trees. The night sky glowed faintly white. Was it from the lights from downtown? Or had the moon come out?

"The sky has turned such a summer color," her mother said as she, too, looked up. "Chieko, you were born in this house. I didn't give birth to you, but you were born here."

Chieko nodded. Just as she had told Shin'ichi at Kiyomizu Temple, Shige and Takichiro had not stolen her as an infant from beneath the cherry blossoms of Maruyama at night. She had been abandoned as a baby at the entrance gate of the shop. Takichiro had carried her into the house.

That had been twenty years ago. Takichiro, who was then in his thirties, was the kind of man who enjoyed himself on the town. At first, Shige did not believe her husband's story.

"You think you're so clever. That's some geisha's baby you've brought home."

"Don't say such stupid things." Takichiro turned red. "Look at the clothes on her. Is this a geisha's baby? Is it?" he asked, holding the baby out to his wife.

Shige took the baby, pressing her face against its cold cheek.

"What shall we do with it?"

"Let's discuss it in the back. I'm in a daze now."

"It's a newborn."

Takichiro and Shige could not adopt the baby, since the real parents were unknown, but they were able to register her as their own legitimate child. They named her Chieko.

Folk wisdom has it that adopting a baby often induces a mother to bear her own, but Shige could not, so Chieko was raised an only child. So many years had passed that Takichiro and his wife no longer worried themselves about the identity of the real parents. They did not know whether Chieko's real father and mother were alive or dead.

Cleaning up after dinner was simple, a mere disposal of the bamboo leaves and taking care of the bowls. Chieko did it alone.

Then Chieko hid herself in her bedroom in the rear of the second floor, contemplating the books of paintings by Klee and Chagall that her father had brought back from the convent at Saga. She fell asleep, but soon awakened screaming.

"Chieko, Chieko," her mother called from the next room. Before Chieko could answer, the sliding door opened.

"You were having a nightmare, weren't you?" Her mother entered the room. "It was a dream, wasn't it?"

Sitting down by Chieko, she turned on the lamp near Chieko's pillow. Chieko sat up on her futon.

"How terrible. Look at all that sweat." Her mother took a gauze towel from the mirror stand. Chieko let her mother wipe her forehead and neck. Shige thought how beautiful Chieko's white chest was.

"Here, now, under your arms." Shige handed the towel to her daughter.

"Thank you, Mother."

"Was it a frightening dream?"

"Yes. I dreamed I was falling from a high place and it was green all around me. There was no bottom."

"That's a dream everyone has," her mother said, ". . . endlessly falling. You mustn't catch cold. Here, change your nightgown."

Chieko nodded, but still had not regained her composure. She tottered as she tried to stand.

"That's all right. I'll get it for you."

Sitting down, Chieko modestly changed her gown, then began to fold the one she had taken off. "You needn't do that. I'll have to wash it anyway," her mother said, taking the gown and tossing it onto the clothes rack in the corner. Then she sat down again by Chieko's pillow.

"A nightmare like that makes me wonder if you have a fever." She put her palm to her daughter's forehead. Contrary to her expectation, it was cold. "Maybe you're tired after going to Kitayama. What a pathetic-looking face . . . Shall I sleep in here tonight?" Her mother started up to get her bedding.

"Thank you. Please don't worry. Go back to sleep. I'm fine."

"Are you sure?" Shige crawled under the edge of her daughter's covers. Chieko leaned toward her.

"It seems strange, Chieko. You're so big now, you can't sleep with your mother holding you."

Shige soon fell into a peaceful sleep. Chieko put her hand on her mother's shoulder to keep it warm. Then she turned off the light, but she could not sleep.

Chieko's dream had been long. She had told her mother

only the end. The first part was more a state between wakeful-
ness and sleep than a dream. She recalled the pleasant day she
had just spent at Kitayama with Masako. Chieko thought more
intently now of the girl Masako had said resembled her. The
green that she fell through at the end of the dream was probably the recollection of the green of Kitayama.

The Bamboo Cutting Ceremony at Kurama Temple was one
of Takichiro's favorite events. He enjoyed its masculine air.
The ceremony was nothing unusual for Takichiro; he had attended many times since his youth, but this time he was thinking of taking Chieko along. He also thought it might be his
only opportunity to go to Kurama, since expenses would probably prevent the Fire Festival from being held this year at the
temple.

Takichiro was concerned about rain. The ceremony was to
be held on June twentieth, in the middle of the rainy season.
On the nineteenth, it was raining rather heavily even for the
wet season. "If it rains like this tomorrow, let's not go," Takichiro said, as he glanced at the sky.

"Father, I don't mind if it's raining."

"Yes, but . . . ," her father said. "But, of course, if the
weather is bad, well . . ."

It was rainy and wet on June twentieth.

"Close the windows . . . and the doors of the wardrobes.
The cloth will get damp with the humidity," Takichiro told a
clerk.

"Are you giving up on going to Kurama Temple?" Chieko
asked her father.

"They'll have it again next year. Let's call it off. With all the
fog around Kurama Temple . . ."

Those who served at the bamboo cutting were mostly local
villagers, not priests; nevertheless they were referred to as
monks. On the eighteenth, in preparation for the ceremony,

they had lashed four stalks each of the male bamboo and the female bamboo to the logs standing to the left and right of the main hall.

The female bamboo had the root attached, while the male bamboo had the root cut off, but the leaves remaining. Since ancient times, the left side of the hall had been called the Tamba Seat and the right side had been called the Omi Seat.

The turn fell upon a different house each year to participate in the ceremony, the family members wearing traditional dress: a coarse silk kimono that had been handed down for generations, warrior's straw sandals, two swords, a priest's stole and priest's robe, nandina leaves around the waist, and a bamboo cutting knife in a brocade sheath. Led by ritual forerunners, they faced the mountain gate.

It was held at one o'clock in the afternoon.

The Bamboo Cutting Ceremony began with the sound of a priest in traditional clothing blowing a conch shell trumpet.

Two festival children faced the chief priest and spoke in unison, "The Bamboo Cutting Ceremony. Felicitous greetings."

Then the festival children advanced to the seats on the right and left.

"Omi Bamboo. How beauteous."

"Tamba Bamboo. How beauteous."

They praised each.

According to custom, the male bamboo, which had been bound to the logs, was first cut down, then arranged on the ground. The more delicate female bamboo was left as it was.

The festival children then announced to the chief priest, "The Bamboo Rites are completed."

The priests entered the inner sanctuary and chanted the sutras. In place of lotus flowers, summer chrysanthemums were scattered about.

The chief priest came down from the altar and opened a cypress fan, raising and lowering it three times. He then called out, and two people from each side cut the bamboo into three pieces.

Takichiro wanted his daughter to see the bamboo cutting, but just as he was hesitating because of the rain, Hideo entered the lattice door carrying a bundle wrapped in a cloth under his arm.

"I finally finished your daughter's obi," he said.

"Obi?" Takichiro looked puzzled. "My daughter's obi?"

Hideo knelt, politely bowing to the floor.

"A tulip pattern?" Takichiro asked casually.

"No, the pattern you drew at the convent at Saga." Hideo was serious. "I am sorry I was so rude to you. I'm young and rash."

Takichiro was secretly surprised. "What? All you did was show a little spunk. You upbraided me. I should thank you for opening my eyes."

"I wove your obi. I brought it with me."

"What?" Takichiro was extremely surprised. "I crumpled that design into a ball and threw it into the stream by your home."

"You threw it away?" Hideo was daringly calm. "I saw enough of the design when you showed it to me. I memorized it."

"I suppose that's your job." As Takichiro spoke, he knitted his brow. "But Hideo, why did you weave the design I threw away? Why? Why did you weave it?" A feeling that was neither sadness nor anger fomented in his chest. "Wasn't it you, Hideo, who said it showed a discordant heart . . . that it was raging and morbid?"

Hideo was silent.

"You did. And that's why I threw it in the stream when I left your shop."

"Mr. Sada, forgive me." Hideo bowed again, apologizing. "I've done a poor job at weaving your design. I've been tired and irritated."

"I have, too. The convent was quiet, of course, but with only one old nun there except for the women who came by to work, it was lonely . . . very lonely. And besides, my business is in trouble, so I thought over and over about what you said. A wholesaler like me doesn't need to draw designs. Those designs are the work of a faddist."

"I thought about things a great deal, too. And since I met your daughter at the Botanical Garden, I've pondered even more," Hideo said. "Would you like to see the obi? If you don't like it, I want you to cut it to pieces."

"Please show it to me," Takichiro said. "Chieko, Chieko," he called to his daughter, who was sitting next to the clerk at the counter. She walked over to them.

Hideo's thick eyebrows and tightly set mouth gave his face a confident look, but his fingers trembled slightly as he untied the bundle.

Hideo turned to sit facing Chieko, as if he found it difficult to speak to her father.

"Chieko, please take a look at this obi. It's your father's design." He handed her the obi without unrolling it.

Chieko unfolded the edge slightly. "Oh, Father, this was inspired by the Klee book. Did you do it at Saga?" She pulled it over her lap. "It's wonderful."

Takichiro's face was sullen and he did not speak, but secretly he was amazed that Hideo had remembered the design so well.

"Father," Chieko spoke with childlike joy. "It's such a beautiful obi!" She touched the fabric. "You wove it so splendidly," she said to Hideo.

"Thank you." Hideo looked down.

"May I unroll it here and take a look at it?"

"Certainly," Hideo answered.

Chieko stood, spreading the obi out in front of Hideo and her father. She stood looking at the obi, her hands on her father's shoulders.

"What do you think, Father?" Takichiro did not speak, so Chieko encouraged him, "Isn't it beautiful?"

"You really like it?" her father asked.

"Yes. Thank you, Father."

"Look at it more closely," Takichiro said.

"It's an innovative pattern, so it will depend on the kimono, but it's a lovely obi."

"Really? Well, if you like it, you should thank Hideo."

"Hideo, thank you." Chieko knelt behind her father and bowed her head toward Hideo.

"Chieko, does this obi have harmony? . . . of the heart?" her father asked.

"Harmony?" Her father's question took her by surprise. She looked at the obi again. "The harmony would depend on the kimono and the person wearing it, but now clothing that purposely destroys that harmony is coming into style."

Her father nodded. "Actually, Chieko, when I showed this design to Hideo, he told me that it had no harmony. So I threw the design in the stream by his shop."

Chieko was silent.

"Even so, the design I threw away looked just like this obi Hideo has woven. Though the thread color is a bit different from my drawing."

"Mr. Sada, please forgive me." Hideo bowed to the floor. "Chieko, this is a selfish request, but would you try the obi on?"

"With this kimono?" Chieko stood up and wrapped the obi around her waist.

Immediately, Chieko glowed with joy. Takichiro's face relaxed.

"Chieko, this is your father's creation." Hideo's eyes flashed.

The Gion Festival

Chieko left the shop carrying a large market basket. She was to cross Oike Street at the upper end and go on to the shop Yubahan in Fuyamachi, but she stood for a moment on Oike Street gazing at the sky, which blazed like flame from Hieizan across to Kitayama. The hour was too early in the long summer day for a sunset glow; the sky was not a melancholy color. The vast flames spread across the heaven.

"I didn't realize there were such sights as this. This is the first time I have seen anything like it."

Chieko took out a small mirror and looked at her own face reflected amid the colors of the clouds.

"I won't forget this. For all my life, I'll never forget this. . . . Man is certainly an emotional creature."

Touched by the color, Hieizan and Kitayama appeared a deep blue.

At Yubahan they sold dried tofu, peony tofu, and stuffed tofu.

"Miss, please come in. We've been so busy with the Gion Festival. I'm sorry we've neglected our old regular patrons. Please forgive me."

Normally the shop only prepared items on order. Kyoto had a number of such businesses among the confectioners and other shops.

"Is this for the Gion Festival? I certainly should thank you for coming here regularly for so many years." The lady filled Chieko's basket almost to overflowing.

Stuffed tofu, just like stuffed eel, contained burdock. Peony tofu resembled a fried mixture of tofu and vegetables, but there were also gingko nuts wrapped inside.

Although this shop was over two hundred years old, the owner had made only a few changes: Glass had been fitted in the small skylight and the Korean-style hearth where the tofu was prepared was now made of brick.

"We used to burn charcoal, but when we would stir up the fire, the cinders made spots on the tofu, so instead we decided to use sawdust."

The woman deftly used bamboo chopsticks to lift the tofu out of square partitioned copper pots, placing it on a slender rod as the upper surface of the tofu began to harden. There were many rods above and below that were raised as the tofu dried.

Chieko went to the rear of the workplace and put her hand on the old pillar. Her mother would always stroke the ancient black pillar when she came to the shop with Chieko.

"What kind of wood is this?" Chieko asked.

"It's cypress. Very tall . . . and perfectly straight."

Touching the pillar again, Chieko could sense its antiquity. Then she left the shop.

As Chieko returned home, the sounds of a Gion Festival band grew louder.

Tourists who came from afar were apt to think that the Gion Festival consisted of only the parade of floats on the seventeenth of July. Many also came to Hieizan on the night of the sixteenth.

But the real ceremonies of the Gion Festival continued all through July. In the various districts in Kyoto, each of which had its own Gion float, the festival bands began to perform and the amulet rituals commenced on the first of July.

Floats with festival children led the procession each year. On July second or third the mayor drew lots to determine the order of the floats. The festival cars were assembled the previous day, but the ceremony of the washing of the shrine palanquins was the true preparatory rite of the festival. The palanquins were washed at the Great Bridge at Shijo over the Kamo River. Although it was called a washing, the Shinto priest simply dipped a *sakaki* branch into the water and sprinkled it on the palanquins.

Then on the eleventh, the festival children visited the Gion Shrine. They were the children who would ride the festival float. Astride horses and wearing the high headdress of a nobleman, the children were accompanied by attendants to the shrine where they were to be granted the fifth court rank. Those above the fifth rank were referred to as imperial court nobles.

In ancient times, the Shinto gods and Buddhist gods became intermingled, so the attendants to the left and right of the festival children were likened to Kannon and Seishi, two boddhisattvas of Buddhism, even though the festival was a Shinto event. The festival children's receiving a court rank from the gods had been compared to the rites of marriage.

"That's bizarre," Shin'ichi had said when he was chosen to be a festival boy. "I'm a man."

The festival children were all required to keep the rite of the "separate fire." In other words, they were to be given food prepared over a special fire apart from that of their families. The purpose was purification, but by now the ritual had been abbreviated to the point where the festival children's food was merely touched by a Shinto purification flame. Rumor was that the festival child would often remind his family, crying "purification fire" when someone absentmindedly forgot to keep the ritual.

The role of the festival children was not easy, since it did not end simply with the one day of the procession. They also had to go around to the many districts making official greetings.

Both the festival itself and the festival children's term lasted almost a full month.

The people of Kyoto savored the elegant mood about Hiei-zan on the sixteenth even more than the procession of floats on July seventeenth.

The day of gathering at Gion had arrived. At Sada's shop they had removed the lattice door, busy with preparations for the festival.

The Gion Festival was held annually at the shrine and so it was nothing unusual for Chieko; she was a Kyoto girl, and on top of that, living near Shijo, she was a parishioner of Yasaka Shrine. It was a festival of the sultry Kyoto summer.

Chieko's fondest memory was seeing Shin'ichi riding on a float as a festival boy. At festival time, whenever she heard the Gion bands and saw the floats surrounded by lanterns, the memory of Shin'ichi would come back to life. Both Shin'ichi and Chieko had been about seven or eight years old at the time.

"I've never seen a girl as beautiful as that child," someone had said.

Chieko followed Shin'ichi when he went to Gion Shrine to be granted the Fifth Rank of Major General and when he rode on the float in the procession. Shin'ichi came in his festival costume accompanied by two attendants to greet Chieko at the shop. When he called to her, she stared at him, blushing. He wore lip rouge and makeup, but Chieko's face was merely suntanned. The bench at the lattice door was overturned, and Chieko, wearing a red dappled obi with her summer kimono, had been setting off firecrackers with some neighborhood children.

Even now, the image of Shin'ichi as a festival boy lingered in the sound of the Gion bands and the lights of the floats.

"Chieko, would you enjoy going to Hieizan?" her mother asked after dinner.

"What about you?"

"We have customers, so I can't leave."

Chieko quickened her steps as she left the house. It was difficult to pass through the crowds of people at Shijo. But Chieko knew where all the floats were located, so she was able to take in all the gay sights in one round. She could hear the music of the many festival bands on the floats.

Chieko walked to the front of Goryosho and bought a candle, lighting it to offer to the deity of the shrine. For the duration of the festival the god of Yasaka was temporarily enshrined in Goryosho, which was located on the south side of Shijo Street at Shinkyogoku.

Chieko noticed a girl at Goryosho who seemed to be performing the "seven-turn worship." She had only seen her from the back, but she realized immediately what the girl was doing. The seven-turn worship involved walking a distance away from the altar before the deity, then returning and bowing, repeating the sequence seven times. During the course of the ritual the worshiper was not to speak even if he happened to see an acquaintance.

Chieko thought she had seen the girl before. Feeling somehow impelled, Chieko, too, began to perform the seven-turn worship.

The girl went to the west and returned to Goryosho. Chieko, however, walked to the east. But the girl's prayers were longer and more sincere than Chieko's.

Chieko did not walk as far as the girl, so they completed the ritual at about the same time.

The girl finally noticed Chieko and stared as if she would swallow her.

"What did you pray for?" Chieko asked.

"Were you watching me?" The girl's voice trembled. "I wanted to know where my sister had gone. You are my sister. God has brought us together." The girl's eyes overflowed with tears.

It was the girl from the Kitayama cedar village.

The altar glowed in the light of the lanterns strung about Goryosho and the candles offered by the worshipers, but the girl's tears took no notice of the brightness.

The flickering light rested on the girl.

Chieko stood firm, her resolve seething within her. "I'm an only child. I have no sisters," she said, but her face turned ashen.

The Kitayama girl sobbed, "I understand. Miss, please forgive me. Forgive me. Ever since I was small . . . my sister . . . I've wondered what's become of my sister. I've made a terrible mistake."

Chieko did not speak.

"I was a twin, but I don't know if I'm older or younger."

"It's just a chance resemblance, don't you think?"

The girl nodded, but tears ran down her cheeks. Taking out a handkerchief and wiping her face, she asked, "Miss, where were you born?"

"In the wholesalers' neighborhood near here."

"Oh! What did you pray for?"

"For the health and happiness of my father and mother."

The girl did not speak.

"And your father?" Chieko asked.

"A long time ago he slipped and fell when he tried to jump from one tree to another while cutting branches in the Kitayama cedars. He hit in a bad place. That's what the people in the village say. I don't know for myself; I had just been born at the time."

Chieko felt her heart had been pierced.

The desire to go to the village and look upon beautiful Kitayama—was it the call of her father's spirit?

The mountain girl had also said she was a twin. Had her real father abandoned the one twin, Chieko, and then, lost in thought in the tops of the cedars, had he slipped and fallen? Certainly it must have happened that way.

Cold sweat oozed from Chieko's forehead. The sound of feet and the music from the Gion bands overflowing from Shijo Street faded in the distance. Chieko's eyes began to turn dark.

The mountain girl put her hand on Chieko's shoulder and wiped Chieko's forehead with a handkerchief.

"Thank you." Chieko wiped her own face with the handkerchief and put it in her own pocket. She did not realize what she had done.

"And what about your mother?" Chieko spoke softly.

"She's dead, too," her voice faltered. "I was born in my mother's village farther back in the mountains than the cedar village. But now my mother is gone, too."

Chieko stopped asking questions.

The Kitayama girl's tears were, of course, tears of joy, and when they stopped her face beamed. But Chieko's heart was so confused that her legs trembled when she tried to stand. This was not an experience she could come to terms with on the spot. The mountain girl's robust beauty was the only thing that seemed to be supporting Chieko. It was impossible for her to be as meekly joyous as the Kitayama girl; a tinge of sorrow deepened in Chieko's eyes.

As Chieko was puzzling over what to do, the mountain girl put out her hand. Chieko took it. The skin was rough and chapped, unlike Chieko's soft hand, but the mountain girl clasped Chieko's hand, seemingly unconcerned about the difference.

"Good-bye, Miss."

"What?"

"Oh. I'm so happy."

"What's your name?"

"Naeko."

"Naeko? My name is Chieko."

"I'm an apprentice now. If you ask for Naeko, anyone would know me right away; it's a small village."

Chieko nodded.

"Miss, are you happy?"

"Yes, I am."

"I won't tell anyone we met tonight. I swear. Only the god of the Gion Shrine will know."

Naeko understood that, although they were twins, their stations in life were different. Chieko did not know what to say, realizing that Naeko had perceived the disparity. But it was Chieko who had been abandoned as a baby.

"Good-bye, Miss," Naeko said. "Hurry, before someone notices us."

Chieko was choked for a response. "Naeko, my family's shop is nearby. At least pass by that way with me."

Naeko shook her head. "What about the people there?"

"My family? It's just my father and mother."

"I don't know why, but somehow I thought that is how it would be. I'm sure you grew up with their love."

Chieko pulled at Naeko's sleeve. "A long time passed before we reached this point."

"Yes, it has."

Naeko then turned back to Goryosho and bowed respectfully. Chieko hurriedly followed.

"Good-bye," Naeko said for the third time.

"Good-bye," said Chieko.

"I have so much to talk to you about. Please come to my village someday. No one would see us in the cedar grove."

"Thank you."

The two of them somehow threaded their way toward Shijo Grand Bridge through the crowds of parishioners of Yasaka Shrine. Although the parades of the seventeenth had ended, the later festivals continued. The stores were open with painted screens set out for decoration. There were early *ukiyoe*, Kano School and Yamato paintings and Sotatsu folding screens. Among the original *ukiyoe* there were some European screens, as well as foreigners depicted in the elegant Kyoto style that expressed the height of vitality of the Kyoto merchant class.

Now that vigor remains in the procession floats, which are decorated with imported Chinese brocade and homespun, Gobelin tapestries, gold-brocaded satin, damask, and embroidered cloth, examples of the splendor of the Momoyama Period, when beautiful articles reached Japan through foreign trade. The insides of the floats were also decorated with famous paintings. Tradition held that the pillarlike structures at the head of the floats had originally been masts on trading ships authorized by the shogun.

A Gion band passed by, playing a simple melody that it was famous for, but there were actually twenty-six musical numbers. The band resembled a Mibu Kyogen, or court music ensemble.

Jostled in the crowd as she approached the bridge, Chieko fell behind Naeko.

Naeko had said good-bye three times, but Chieko was not certain whether they had already parted or whether Naeko would walk with her past the shop so she could show her where she lived. She felt a warm closeness to Naeko that filled her heart.

"Chieko!" Hideo came up, calling to Naeko just as she was about to cross the bridge. Mistaking her for Chieko, he asked, "Did you go to Hieizan? . . . alone?"

Naeko stopped, but she did not look back at Chieko.

Chieko quickly hid behind some people.

"The weather's nice, isn't it?" Hideo said to Naeko. "To-morrow will be nice, too. The stars are so bright."

Naeko looked up at the sky, at a loss for a reply. Naeko, of course, could not have known Hideo.

"I'm sorry I was so rude to your father the other day. Was the obi all right?"

"Yes."

"Your father felt offended later, didn't he?"

"Uh . . . yes." Not knowing what he was talking about,

Naeko did not know how to answer. Even so, she never glanced back at Chieko.

Naeko was puzzled. If it were all right that Chieko should speak to the young man, then Chieko should approach them.

The young man had a rather large head, broad shoulders, and deep-set eyes. To Naeko he did not look like a bad fellow. His talk of obis led her to think he was a weaver from Nishijin. After years of sitting at a loom, one's body comes to have a particular look about it.

"I'm young. I spoke out of turn about your father's design. But I thought about it overnight and decided to weave it," Hideo said.

Naeko did not respond.

"Have you worn it?"

"Well . . . yes," Naeko replied.

"How was it?"

The light was not as bright on the bridge as in the street, and the bustling crowds threatened to separate the two of them. Still Naeko found it strange that Hideo should mistake her for Chieko. Twins who grew up in the same family are sometimes difficult to distinguish, but Chieko and Naeko had led completely different lives in different places. Naeko wondered if the young man might be nearsighted.

"Chieko, I have a plan. I want to put all my energy into weaving an obi that would be a keepsake for your twenties."

"Oh . . . thank you," Naeko's voice faltered.

"Having met you here at Gion, perhaps I'll have divine help in weaving your obi."

Naeko did not speak. The only thing that Naeko could imagine was that Chieko did not want the young man to know they were twins, and that was why she would not come to their side.

"Good-bye," Naeko said. Hideo thought it was rather abrupt.

"Oh . . . good-bye," he answered. "Please let me make the

obi for you. Is it all right? Maybe we can meet again during the maple season."

Naeko looked around for Chieko, but she could not find her.

The young man and his talk of obis did not bother Naeko; she was happy simply thinking that meeting Chieko in front of the Goryosho was a blessing from God. She held onto the bridge railing and gazed for a moment at the reflections of the lanterns in the water. Then she walked slowly along the side of the bridge. She planned to visit Yasaka Shrine at the end of Shijo.

As she approached the middle of the bridge, she noticed Chieko talking with two young men.

"Oh," she cried out in a small voice, although she was alone. She did not approach them, but she found herself watching in spite of herself.

Chieko had wondered what Naeko and Hideo could have been talking about. Hideo had obviously mistaken Naeko for Chieko, but surely Naeko had been flustered, not knowing how to respond to the young man.

It might have been better to approach them, but Chieko had not. And not only that; when Hideo had called out to Naeko, Chieko had promptly concealed herself in the crowd. Why had she done so?

The jolt of meeting in front of Goryosho was far more intense for Chieko than for Naeko. Naeko had said that she already knew she was a twin and had looked for her sister. But Chieko had never even dreamed of such a thing, and this was all too sudden. She was not prepared to feel the joy that Naeko had felt. This was the first time she heard that her real father had fallen from a cedar and that her real mother, too, had died young. It pierced her heart.

Chieko had caught the neighbors' whispers and realized that she was a foundling, but she had forced herself not to wonder about what sort of parents had abandoned her. She could not have known even if she had given thought to it. Besides, Takichiro and Shige's love for her had been so warm, she saw no need to pursue her origins.

It was not necessarily a fortunate experience for Chieko, hearing what Naeko had to say this evening at Hieizan, but it seemed that Naeko would develop a tender love for her sister.

"Your heart is purer than mine. You work hard, and your body is strong," Chieko whispered. "Someday will I need your help?"

In a daze, Chieko had been crossing Shijo Bridge when Shin'ichi called to her, "Why are you walking around alone looking so bewildered? Your color isn't very good."

"Oh, Shin'ichi." Chieko seemed to come to her senses. "You were so cute when you rode on the float as a festival boy."

"It was a terrible experience at the time, but when I look back on it now I have good memories."

Shin'ichi had someone with him. "This is my older brother. He's in graduate school."

The brother resembled Shin'ichi. He bowed his head brusquely.

"When Shin'ichi was little he was a crybaby and cute like a girl. That's why they made him a festival boy. What an idiot," Shin'ichi's brother laughed loudly.

They had come halfway across the bridge. Chieko looked at the older brother's manly face.

"Chieko, you look pale tonight. And you seem terribly sad," Shin'ichi said.

"It's probably just the light here in the middle of the bridge," Chieko said as she stepped firmly. "Besides, everyone here at Hieizan is having a good time, so naturally a girl alone would look sad."

"That won't do." Shin'ichi led Chieko to the bridge railing. "Just lean here a moment."

"Thank you."

"There isn't much of a breeze on the river."

Chieko put her hand to her forehead and seemed about to close her eyes. "Shin'ichi, how old were you when you rode on the float as a festival boy?"

"Let's see . . . was I seven? I think it was the year before I went to elementary school."

Chieko nodded, but did not speak. Cold sweat began to appear on her forehead and neck. She put her hand in her pocket and found Naeko's handkerchief there. It was wet with Naeko's tears. Chieko did not know what to do. Should she take it out or not? She wadded it in her palm and wiped her forehead. She was almost moved to tears.

Shin'ichi was suspicious. He knew it was not Chieko's nature to leave an old handkerchief in her pocket.

"Chieko, are you hot? Or do you have a chill? A summer cold can be difficult to shake . . . if that's what it is. You'd better go home right away. We'll take you . . . won't we, Ryusuke?"

His brother nodded. He had been looking at Chieko the whole time.

"It's nearby. You don't have to."

"Yes, it is close, but that's all the more reason to go with you," Shin'ichi's brother spoke firmly.

The three of them walked back from the middle of the bridge.

"Shin'ichi, did you know that I followed the float that you were riding on in the procession as a festival boy?" Chieko asked.

"Yes, I knew. I remember it well," Shin'ichi answered.

"We were so little then."

"Yes, we were. It's unsightly for a festival child to be looking off to the side while he's riding in a procession. Even so, I thought I saw a little girl following me. You must have got tired, being pushed around in the crowd."

"I wasn't that little."

"What do you mean?" Shin'ichi parried lightly. He wondered what had happened to Chieko tonight. When they arrived at Chieko's shop, Shin'ichi's brother greeted Chieko's parents politely. Shin'ichi hid behind his brother's back.

Takichiro was drinking festival sake with a guest in the back room. They were not so much drinking as they were enjoying one another's company. Shige was up and down waiting on them.

"I'm home," Chieko said.

"You're early." Shige looked at her daughter. Chieko greeted her father's guest.

"Mother, I'm sorry I was too late to help out here."

"That's all right." Shige signaled to her daughter with her eye, and the two of them went into the kitchen, ostensibly to get a bottle of sake. "Chieko, those boys brought you home because you look so helpless, didn't they?"

"Yes, Shin'ichi and his brother . . ."

"Well, your color looks bad, and you seem unsteady on your feet." Shige put her palm to Chieko's forehead. "You don't seem to have a fever, but you look so sad. Tonight we have a guest, so you can sleep with me." She softly hugged Chieko's shoulders. Chieko held back a tear.

"You go on upstairs in the back to sleep."

"I will, thank you." Chieko's heart softened at her mother's kindness.

"Your father has been a bit lonely since he doesn't have many guests . . . though we did have five or six here for dinner."

Chieko carried the sake holder to the parlor.

"I've had plenty, thank you. Just this one more will be enough."

The container shook as she poured the sake, so she used her left hand as well. Still, her hands trembled. Tonight a light had been put in the Christian lantern. She could faintly see the violets growing in the two hollows of the great maple.

There were no flowers on them now, but the two small violets in the upper and lower hollows—were they Chieko and Naeko? It looked as though the violets could never meet, but had they met tonight? As Chieko looked at the violets in the dim light, she was again moved to tears.

Takichiro, too, noticed something about Chieko. He glanced at her occasionally.

Chieko stood up quietly and went upstairs. The guest bedding had been laid out in her usual room. Taking a pillow from the drawer, Chieko got into her futon.

She buried her face in the pillow and held the edges so no one would hear her crying.

Shige came upstairs and noticed that Chieko's pillow was wet. "You can tell me about it later," she said as she took out a new pillow and immediately started back down. Pausing at the head of the stairs, she looked back, but said nothing.

It was not that three futons would not fit in the room, but only two had been taken out. One was Chieko's; it seemed her mother had planned to sleep with her. Two linen summer top sheets, Chieko's and her mother's, lay folded at the foot of the futon. Shige had prepared her daughter's bed for her. It was a small act, but Chieko was moved by her mother's kindness. With that, her tears stopped, and her heart was calmed.

"This is my home."

It was only natural that Chieko would not be able to control the confusion in her heart on meeting Naeko so suddenly.

Chieko stood in front of the mirror stand, looking at her

own face. She considered putting on some makeup, but decided against it. She simply took a bottle of perfume and sprinkled the tiniest bit on the bedding. Then she adjusted her undersash.

Of course, sleep did not come easily.

"I wonder if I was cruel to Naeko."

When she closed her eyes, she could see the beautiful cedar mountains of Nakagawa Village.

From what Naeko had told her, Chieko had learned the facts about her real parents.

"Would it be better to tell my father and mother or not?"

Most likely Chieko's parents here at the shop knew nothing of the place where Chieko was born or of her real father and mother.

Even the thought that they were no longer in this world did not bring tears to Chieko's eyes.

The sound of a Gion band drifted in from the town.

The guest downstairs seemed to be a crepe dealer from somewhere near Nagahama in Omi. The sake had made several rounds, so their voices were rather loud. Snatches of the conversation reached Chieko where she lay in the rear of the second floor.

The guest stubbornly insisted that the reason the float procession now began at Shijo, went down the wide, very modern Kawaramachi, turned down Oike, and passed in front of City Hall was for the sake of tourism.

Previously the parade had followed the narrow streets typical of Kyoto—streets so narrow, in fact, that occasionally houses were damaged by the passing floats. Back then the procession had a grace to it. One could even receive a rice cake by reaching out from a second-story window as a float passed the house.

When the floats turned off Shijo onto the narrow streets, one could not see the skirts of the floats, which was good.

Takichiro defended the new way, explaining that he thought it was splendid now to be able to see the whole float easily on the wider streets.

Lying in the bedroom, even now Chieko could almost hear the sound of the floats' great wooden wheels turning at a cross-road.

It seemed the guest would be staying in the next room tonight. Tomorrow Chieko planned to tell her mother and father everything she had heard from Naeko.

All the businesses in Kitayama village were family enterprises, but not all the houses owned part of the mountain. In fact, few did. Chieko thought her parents had probably been employed by one of the landowning houses.

Naeko had said that she was herself apprenticed.

Twenty years ago it was not just that her parents would have been embarrassed at having twins, but it would also have been difficult to raise them both. Perhaps they had abandoned Chieko wondering how they could live otherwise.

Chieko had failed to ask Naeko three things. Chieko had been abandoned as an infant, but why had they abandoned Chieko and not Naeko? When had her father fallen from the tree? Naeko had said it was right after they were born. She had also mentioned that they were born in their mother's village further back in the mountains. What was the name of the place?

Chieko's social status had changed when she was abandoned, so Naeko seemed to think, and now she could never come to call on Chieko. If Chieko wanted to talk to her, she would have to go to Naeko's cedar mountains.

But it seemed that Chieko could no longer go without letting her parents know.

Chieko had read over and over the beautiful passage from *The Temptation of Kyoto* by Osaragi Jiro: "The planted groves of cedars destined to be made into Kitayama logs stand with their branches layered one atop another like stratus clouds, while the mountains themselves are delicately linked together by the trunks of the red pines. And they send out, like music, the singing voices of the trees." These words came to mind.

The music of the round mountains, each enjoined to the next, and the singing voices of the trees communicated with her heart, even more than the bands and the other festivities. It was as if she heard the music and the singing through the rainbows that often appeared over Kitayama.

Chieko's sadness faded. Perhaps it had not been sadness. Maybe it was the surprise, the puzzlement, the distress of meeting Naeko so suddenly. But perhaps it is a girl's fate to shed tears.

As she turned over and closed her eyes, Chieko listened to the mountain's song.

"Naeko was overjoyed, but what did I do?"

Shortly, her father and mother came upstairs with the guest. "Sleep well," Takichiro told him.

Chieko's mother folded the clothes the guest took off, then came to the room Chieko was in and began to fold Takichiro's. "I'll do it, Mother," Chieko said.

"Are you still awake?" She left them to Chieko and lay down. "It smells good here. You're young," she said.

Soon the guest from Omi could be heard snoring on the other side of the sliding panel door, probably thanks to the sake.

"Shige," Takichiro called to his wife in the next room. "Don't you think that Mr. Arita wants to send his son to our shop?"

"As a clerk . . . or some kind of employee?"

"As a husband for Chieko."

"Such talk! Chieko isn't asleep yet," Shige said to silence her husband.

"I know. It's all right if she hears."

Chieko did not speak.

"It's his second son. He's come here several times on errands."

"I don't like Mr. Arita very well," Shige spoke in a hushed voice, but firmly.

Chieko's mountain music vanished.

"Isn't that right, Chieko?" Her mother turned over toward her. Chieko opened her eyes, but did not answer. For a while it was quiet. Chieko rested one ankle on top of the other and lay still.

"Arita wants this shop . . . I think he does anyway," Takichiro said. "He knows that Chieko is a good and beautiful girl. And he understands our business quite well. We have some employees who tell everything in detail."

No one spoke.

"Well, it doesn't matter how beautiful Chieko is—I've never even considered marrying her off for business, have I, Shige? God wouldn't forgive me."

"That's right," Shige said.

"My disposition just isn't right for this shop."

"Father, forgive me for having you take those books of Paul Klee's paintings to the convent at Saga." Chieko got up and apologized to her father.

"What? They're my pleasure . . . my comfort. They're what I live for now." Her father bowed his head slightly. "Though I don't have the talent for such designs."

"Father."

"Chieko, if I sold this shop—Nishijin would be all right—but if we moved to a small, quiet house near Nanzenji or Okazaki, and the two of us thought up designs for kimono cloth and obis, how would that be? Could you stand being poor?"

"Poor? I wouldn't mind at all."

With that her father finally seemed to doze off, but Chieko could not sleep.

The next morning Chieko got up early, swept the street in front of the shop, and wiped the benches at the lattice door.

The Gion Festival continued.

After the eighteenth there was the building of the festival floats, then the Festival of Screens at Hieizan on the twenty-third, the procession of floats on the twenty-fourth, and after that, the dedicatory *kyogen* performance, the shrine palanquin washing on the twenty-eighth, then back at Yasaka Shrine there was a festival to announce the end of the Shinto ceremonies.

Several of the floats passed through Teramachi.

With all the activity of the month of festivals, Chieko's heart would not be calmed.

The Color of Autumn

One of the last reminders still left in Kyoto of the "opening of civilization" of the Meiji Period—the electric streetcar that ran along the Horikawa Kitano line—was finally to be dismantled.

The thousand-year-old capital was known as a place where many of the innovations from the West were promptly adopted. This trait was evident among many of the people of Kyoto.

But perhaps there is still something of the old capital in a city that would keep the streetcar running so long. Naturally, the train itself was small; one's knees almost touched those of the person sitting opposite.

Now that the streetcar was to be dismantled, however, it seemed everyone hated to part with it. People decorated it with blossoms, calling it the "flower train." The streetcar was advertised with passengers dressed in the fashion of the Meiji Period. Would this become another Kyoto festival?

The train continued to run for many days with a full load of passengers who had no particular reason for riding. It was July, and some even carried parasols.

The summer sun in Kyoto is much more intense than in Tokyo, where nowadays one seldom saw anyone carrying a parasol.

As Takichiro was preparing to board the "flower train" in front of Kyoto station, a middle-aged woman standing behind him was trying to stifle a smile. Takichiro did have somewhat of a Meiji air about him that would qualify him to ride the old train.

Takichiro noticed the woman as he got on the train. He

spoke rather embarrassedly, "What do you mean, laughing? You don't have any Meiji credentials."

"I'm not too far removed from that era," the woman answered. "Besides, I live along the Kitano line."

"Really? Oh, yes, that was the place," Takichiro said.

" 'That was the place'! What a cold way to put it! Even so, you were kind enough to remember."

"That's a pretty girl you have with you. Where were you hiding her?"

"Fool. She's not my child. You should know that."

"Well, I didn't. You know how women are."

"What do you mean? . . . It's a man's problem, too."

The girl, about fourteen or fifteen, had beautiful white skin. Over her light summer kimono she wore a narrow red obi. She was shy. Pursing her lips, she sat next to the woman in order to avoid Takichiro.

Takichiro tugged lightly on the woman's sleeve.

"Sit here between us," the woman told the girl.

For a moment the three of them said nothing. Then the woman leaned over the girl's head and whispered into Takichiro's ear.

"I'm thinking about sending her to be a *maiko* at Gion."

"Whose child is she?"

"She's the daughter of a tearoom owner nearby."

"I see."

"Some people say she must belong to you and me," the woman spoke in a voice Takichiro could barely hear.

"What!"

The woman was the proprietress of a tearoom at Kamishichiken.

"We're on our way to the Kitano Tenjin Shrine. The girl wanted to go."

Takichiro realized that the woman was joking.

"How old are you?" he asked the girl.

"I'm in the first year of middle school."

"Hmm." Takichiro looked at the girl. "Well, I'll call on you after you're reborn in that other world."

It seemed that Takichiro's strange words would reach only a child of the gay quarters.

"Why must you go to the Kitano Shrine with her? Is she an incarnation of Tenjin?" Takichiro teased the proprietress.

"She is. She is."

"But Tenjin was male."

"Reincarnated as a girl." The woman disposed of Takichiro's protest. "It's because if he were reincarnated as a man he'd suffer the bitterness of exile again."

Takichiro almost burst out laughing. "And as a woman?"

"As a woman, well . . . as a woman, one is loved and cared for by a lover."

"I see."

The girl was indisputably beautiful. Her black hair glistened, the color of some mysterious water creature. She was a lovely girl, whose eyes had almost a Western appearance.

"Is she an only child?" Takichiro asked.

"No, she has two older sisters. The older one will finish middle school next spring, so she might make her debut then."

"Is she beautiful like this girl?"

"She resembles her, but she's not as beautiful as this one."

There was not a single *maiko*, an apprentice geisha, in Kamishichiken now. Even if a girl were to become a *maiko*, it was not permitted until after she finished middle school.

Kamishichiken, or the "Upper Seven Houses," was so called because originally there had been only seven teahouses there. Takichiro had heard that the number had increased to twenty.

In the past, not so long ago, Takichiro often used to go to Kamishichiken for pleasure, accompanied by weavers from Nishijin or his favorite customers from outlying areas. His shop was prospering then.

"You must be quite inquisitive yourself . . . riding this train and all."

"It's essential that people should hate to part with things," she said. "Our business doesn't forget old patrons."

Takichiro was silent.

"Besides, today I just saw a guest off to Kyoto station. This train line is on our way home. Isn't it you, Mr. Sada, who's a bit odd . . . riding all alone?"

"Maybe so. I wonder why I am. It should have been enough just to see the flower train." Takichiro inclined his head. "Is it that the past is so full of memories? Or is it because it's so lonely now?"

"Lonely? I'm not so old as to talk like that. Won't you come with us? If only to see the young girls?"

Takichiro felt as though he would be escorted to Kamishichiken.

Takichiro followed the proprietress as she walked directly to the altar of the Kitano Shrine. Her meticulous prayer was long. The girl, too, bowed her head. The woman returned to Takichiro's side. "Please excuse her."

"Certainly."

"You go on home now," the woman spoke to the girl.

"Thank you." The girl said good-bye to the two of them. As she walked away, her gait took on the look of a middle school student.

"You seem to have taken quite a liking to the girl," the woman said. "She'll make her debut in about two or three years. You can look forward to it, but it will be difficult to wait. She's so beautiful."

Takichiro did not respond. Having come this far, he wanted to walk around the grounds, but it was hot.

"Could I take a rest at your place? I've become quite tired."

"Of course. I was planning on it from the start. It's been a long time," the woman said.

As they approached the old teahouse, the proprietress spoke again. "Come inside. What have you been doing lately? I've heard rumors about you. Please lie down, and I'll bring a pillow. You mentioned being lonely. I'll bring a gentle girl you can talk with."

"I don't want to see any of the geisha I've met before."

A young geisha came in just as Takichiro was beginning to doze. She sat quietly for a moment, probably wondering about this troubled guest whom she was meeting for the first time. Takichiro sat languidly, making no attempt to enliven the conversation. The geisha spoke, trying to cheer him. She said that since she made her debut she had met some forty-seven men who struck her fancy.

"Just like in the famous old play about the forty-seven loyal retainers. It's funny to think about it now—falling for so many men. Some were in their forties or fifties. Everyone laughed at me."

Takichiro woke up completely. "And now?"

"Now, just one."

The proprietress was also in the parlor.

The geisha was about twenty years old. Still, Takichiro wondered if she really remembered all forty-seven men even though she had had no deep relationship with them.

Once, only three days after her debut, a guest suddenly kissed her as she was showing him to the restroom. She bit his tongue.

"Did he bleed?"

"Yes, he did. He told us to pay his doctor's fee. The man was terribly angry. I cried and there was a little disturbance. But it was his fault. . . . Don't you think so? I've already forgotten his name."

"Hmm." Takichiro looked at the geisha's face, imagining the sloping-shouldered, seemingly gentle beauty suddenly biting hard on someone's tongue.

"Show me your teeth," Takichiro told the geisha.

"Teeth? My teeth? Didn't you see them while I was talking?"

"I want to get a better look."

"No. I'm embarrassed." The geisha kept her lips closed. "I wouldn't be able to talk."

The geisha's teeth were like white beads in her beautiful mouth. Takichiro teased her, "I know. Your teeth broke then, and these are false, aren't they?"

"A tongue is soft, so . . . ," she said absentmindedly. "Oh, stop it." She hid her head behind the proprietress.

After a while, Takichiro spoke up, "I've come this far, so I think I'll drop by Nakasato."

"What? They'd be happy to see you there. May I go with you?" The proprietress stood up. Then she sat for a moment before the mirror.

Nakasato had the original front on the building, but the guestrooms inside were all new.

Another geisha joined them. Takichiro stayed at Nakasato until after dinner.

Hideo came to the shop while Takichiro was out. He had told Chieko to meet him there, so she was waiting out front.

"I finished the design for the obi I promised at the Gion Festival. I came to have you take a look at it," Hideo said.

"Chieko," her mother called. "Why don't you two go sit in the back?"

"All right."

Hideo showed the design to Chieko as they sat in the room that faced the inner garden. There were two designs. One was of chrysanthemums arranged among leaves. It was rendered in such a novel way that one did not recognize them as chrysanthemum leaves. The other design was of maples.

"They're lovely." Chieko admired them.

"I'm happy you like them," Hideo said. "Which one shall I weave for you?"

"Well, I could wear the chrysanthemums all year."

"So, shall I use the chrysanthemum pattern?"

Chieko did not speak. She looked down. Her face took on a concerned look.

"Both of them are fine, but . . . " Her voice faltered. "Could you make a design of mountains with cedars and red pines?"

"Mountains with red pines and cedars? It sounds as if it would be difficult, but I could think about it." Hideo gave Chieko a smoldering look.

"Hideo, I'm sorry."

"Sorry? There's nothing to be sorry about."

"But it . . . " Chieko searched for words. "It wasn't me you promised the obi to on the bridge at Shijo at the festival. You mistook someone else for me."

Hideo's voice would not come out; he could not believe her. His face lost its strength. It was for Chieko that he had put his whole heart into the design. Was it Chieko's intention to reject Hideo completely?

But if that were the case, Hideo could comprehend neither Chieko's objections nor her manner. He recovered his violent emotion.

"Did I meet your ghost? Was it your ghost I talked to? Do ghosts appear at the Gion Festival?" Hideo did not mention the old superstition of seeing the phantom of one's beloved.

Chieko's face tightened. "Hideo, the girl you talked to was my sister."

Hideo did not speak, so Chieko went on. "She's my sister. I had just met her myself for the first time that night. She's my sister."

He still did not respond.

"I haven't even told my mother and father about her yet."

"What do you mean?" Hideo was taken aback. He did not understand.

"You know the Kitayama log village? She works there."

"What?"

Chieko's confession was so abrupt that Hideo could find no words.

"You know Nakagawa District?" Chieko asked.

"Yes, I've been through there on the bus."

"Give that girl one of your obis."

"What?"

"Please give one to her."

Hideo nodded with a suspicious look, but then asked, "So, did you say you wanted me to make one with a red pine and cedar mountain design?"

Chieko nodded.

"All right. But won't it be too good for a girl like her?"

"It's your responsibility to take that into account. She'll treasure it all her life. Her name is Naeko. She's not a land-owner's daughter, so she works hard. More . . . much more than someone like me."

Hideo was still doubtful. "I'll make the obi, since you've asked me."

"Remember, her name is Naeko."

"I see. But why does she look so much like you?"

"We're sisters."

"But even sisters would not . . . "

She did not reveal to Hideo that they were twins.

It was probably not altogether because his eyes played tricks on him that Hideo mistook Naeko for Chieko in the evening light, since they were wearing light summer festival dress, as was everyone else.

How could they be sisters, Hideo wondered. This girl he saw now before him—the daughter of a fine Kyoto kimono wholesaler whose old-fashioned, somewhat out-of-date shop stood deep in the recesses behind layers of beautiful lattice doors— and an apprenticed girl in a log village in Kitayama. But it was not something he could delve into.

"When I finish the obi, may I bring it here?" Hideo asked.

"Well," Chieko thought for a moment. "Could you deliver it directly to Naeko?"

"Yes, I could."

"Then please do." Chieko's heart was in her request. "It *is* a bit far away."

"I know. But it's easy to find."

"Naeko will be so happy."

"Will she accept it?" Hideo's doubt was reasonable. He wondered if Naeko might be surprised.

"I'll tell her about it."

"Oh, if you'd do that, I'd be happy to deliver it. What's the name of the house?"

Chieko did not know. "The house where she lives?"

"Yes."

"I'll let you know by telephone or in a letter."

"All right," Hideo said. "I'll take it to her. I'll weave it well, as though it were your obi, rather than your double's."

"Thank you." Chieko lowered her head. "Do you think this is all bizarre? I'm sorry to trouble you, but, Hideo, please don't weave it for me. Do it for Naeko."

"I will."

As Hideo left the shop, naturally he felt as though he were wrapped in a puzzle; nevertheless, he had already set his head to work on a pattern. He feared the design would be too plain for Chieko unless he were to make it quite bold. Hideo still seemed to regard it as Chieko's obi. No, if it were Naeko's obi, then he would have to design it in such a manner that it would not clash with her way of life. It was as he had said to Chieko.

Hideo turned his steps toward the bridge at Shijo where he had first met "Chieko's Naeko" or "Naeko's Chieko," but it was hot under the noonday sun. Leaning against the rail at the end of the bridge, he closed his eyes. He listened, not for the echoes of the crowds or the trains, but for the almost imperceptible sound of the flow of the river.

This year Chieko did not see the Daimonji. Her mother even went with her father on a rare outing together, but Chieko stayed home.

Her parents reserved a whole room at a teahouse in Kiya Nijo along with several nearby business friends.

The Daimonji on the sixteenth of August is a fire to mark the end of the Bon Festival. It is said that the custom of lighting a fire on the mountain comes from the tradition of throwing burning torches to guide the spirits through the night sky back to the realm of the dead.

The Daimonji on Niyoigatake Peak on Higashiyama is the best known, but there were actually five mountains where fires were lighted. The "Left Daimonji" on Okitayama near Kinkakuji, the "Myoho" on Mount Matsugasaki, the "Funagata" on Akimiyama in Nishigamo, and the "Toriigata" on a mountain in Kamisaga. In all, five "sending fires" were lighted, bonfires to direct the spirits of the dead back to the netherworld. For the forty minutes of the events, all the neon lighting and advertising in the city was turned off.

Chieko could sense the color of early autumn in the sending fires and glow of the night sky.

About two weeks earlier than the Daimonji, on the evening before the beginning of autumn, the ceremonies of the "summer passing" were held at the Shimogamo Shrine.

Chieko and her friends used to climb the dikes on the Kamo River to view the Left Daimonji. She had been accustomed to seeing the Daimonji since she was a child.

"It's already time for the Daimonji again," the thought came to her heart every year.

Chieko went out to the front of the shop and played with the neighborhood children around the benches. The children seemed to pay no attention to such things as the Daimonji, preferring the more interesting fireworks.

This year the Bon Festival brought a new sadness to Chieko; she had met Naeko at Gion and had been told that her real father and mother had died long ago.

"Yes, I'll go see Naeko tomorrow," Chieko thought. "I'll have to tell her about Hideo's obi."

The next day Chieko went out in inconspicuous clothes. She had never seen Naeko in the daylight.

She got off the bus at Bodai Falls.

It seemed to be the busy season at Kitayama. The men were trimming the rough bark from the cedar logs. It fell all around in piles.

Chieko hesitated, then walked a bit. Suddenly Naeko came running toward her at top speed.

"Miss, thank you for coming. Thank you."

Chieko looked at Naeko's work clothes. "Are you sure it's all right?"

"Yes, I asked for the rest of the day off . . . when I saw you." Naeko spoke between breaths. "Shall we talk in the mountains? No one will see us there." She pulled Chieko's sleeve.

Naeko lightheartedly took off her apron and spread it on the ground. The Tamba cotton apron went all the way around the back so it was wide enough for both girls to sit on together.

"Please, sit down," Naeko said.

"Thank you."

Naeko took the towel off her head and fluffed her hair with her fingers. "Thank you so much for coming. I'm so happy." Her eyes sparkled as she gazed at Chieko.

The scent of the earth and the trees was strong—the fragrances of the cedar mountain.

"If we sit here, no one can see us from below," Naeko said.

"I like the cedar groves. I've come often before, but this is the first time I've ever been up in the mountains." Chieko looked about. The two girls were surrounded by the straight cedar trunks of uniform size.

"These are man-made trees," Naeko said.

"What?"

"These are about forty years old. They'll be cut and made into columns or the like. Left alone, they would probably grow for a thousand years . . . wide and tall. I think about that occasionally. I like virgin forests the best, but in this village it's as though we're growing flowers for cutting."

Chieko did not speak.

"Were there no such thing as man, there would be nothing like Kyoto either. It would all be natural woods and fields of grasses. This land would belong to the deer and wild boar, wouldn't it? Why did man come into this world? It's frightening . . . mankind."

"Naeko, do you think about such things?" Chieko was surprised.

"Yes, sometimes."

"Do you dislike people?"

"I love people," Naeko answered. "I like nothing as much as people, but how would it be if there were no people on earth? I suddenly think of things like that after napping in the mountains."

"Isn't that a kind of pessimism hidden in your heart?"

"I hate pessimism. I enjoy working here every day . . . but I wonder about people. . . ."

The cedar grove suddenly turned dark.

"It's an evening shower," Naeko said. The rain began to collect on the leaves of the cedars, falling in great drops. The violent thunder rumbled.

"I'm frightened." Chieko turned pale. Naeko took her hand.

"Miss, bend your knees and crouch into a ball," Naeko

said, leaning over Chieko, completely covering her with her body.

The thunder became more and more intense until soon there was no interval between the lightning and the thunder. The mountains seemed as though they would be rent with the sound.

The storm was right above the girls.

The branches of the trees on the cedar mountain were astir in the rain. Each time the lightning flashed, it illuminated the earth and glared on the trees around the girls. In that moment the beautiful straight trunks of the trees in the grove appeared uncanny and ominous. Then the thunder crashed.

"Naeko, we're going to be struck!" Chieko huddled smaller.

"It might strike the ground, but it won't hit us," Naeko said firmly. "Do you think lightning would strike you?"

Then she covered Chieko with her body even more completely.

"Miss, your hair got wet." Naeko wiped the back of Chieko's head with her towel. Then she divided Chieko's hair into two strands and wound it up on top of her head.

"A few raindrops may fall, but lightning would never even strike near you."

Chieko calmed at hearing Naeko's kind voice. "Thank you. Thank you so much. But didn't you get wet protecting me?"

"These are my work clothes. I don't mind in the least," Naeko said. "I'm very happy."

"What's that shiny thing on your belt?" Chieko asked.

"Oh, I had forgotten. It's a scythe. I'd been using it to cut bark from the cedars on the roadside when I ran over to meet you." She looked at it. "It's dangerous." She threw the scythe away. It was small, without a wooden handle.

"I'll pick it up on the way back . . . but I don't really want to go."

The thunder seemed to be passing.

Chieko could clearly feel Naeko's embrace as the mountain girl covered her with her body.

Though it was summer, the shower in the mountains made everything cold, but as Naeko covered Chieko from head to foot, the warmth in Naeko's form spread deep into Chieko's body.

The warmth was inexpressible. Chieko held still for a moment, her eyes closed with joyful thoughts.

"Naeko, thank you," she said again. "I wonder if you did this for me in our mother's womb."

"Weren't we pushing and kicking each other around in there?"

"Maybe so," Chieko laughed in an intimate voice.

The shower passed with the thunder.

"Naeko, thank you. I think I'm all right now." Chieko moved as if she would get up.

"Yes, but let's stay like this a while longer. The raindrops that collected on the leaves are still falling." Naeko continued to cover Chieko.

Chieko put her hand on Naeko's back. "You're all wet. Aren't you cold?"

"I'm accustomed to it. It's nothing," Naeko said. "I'm so happy you came. I feel warm inside. You got a bit wet, too."

"Naeko, was this the place where our father fell from the tree?" Chieko asked.

"I don't know. I was only a child then myself."

"Where is our mother's home village? Do we have a grandfather or grandmother?"

"I don't know that either," Naeko answered.

"Weren't you raised in the village?"

"Miss, why do you ask such questions?"

Chieko swallowed her words, hearing Naeko speak so sharply.

"Don't you have a family?" Naeko asked.

Chieko did not answer.

"I would be grateful if you'd think of me as your sister. I'm sorry about what I said at the Gion Festival."

"I was happy."

"I was, too, but I can't go to your home."

"But, if you would, I'd arrange everything . . . I'll talk to my father and mother . . . "

"No," Naeko said firmly. "If you were ever in trouble, as you were just now, I'd go to protect you, even if I would die doing it. You understand, don't you?"

Chieko was moved to tears. "Naeko, you didn't know what to do at the festival that evening when you were mistaken for me, did you?"

"You mean when the man talked to me about the obi?"

"He's a weaver at an obi shop in Nishijin. He said he'd make an obi for you, didn't he?"

"Because he mistook me for you."

"The other day he came to show me the design. I told him it wasn't me. I told him it was my sister."

"What?"

"I asked him to make an obi for my sister, Naeko, too."

"For me?"

"Didn't he promise you he would?"

"But he had mistaken me for you."

"He's making one for me and one for you, too . . . as a token that we are sisters."

"Me?" Naeko was taken aback.

"It was a promise made at Gion, wasn't it?" Chieko asked softly.

Even as she continued to cover Chieko, Naeko's body became stiff, but she didn't move.

"Chieko, if you were ever in trouble, I would gladly take

your place, but I can't accept a gift in your stead. It would be shameful."

"It's not a vicarious gift."

"It is."

How could Chieko persuade her?

"Wouldn't you accept it if I were to give it to you?"

Naeko did not answer.

"I'm having him weave it so I can give it to you."

"That's not the way it was. On the night of the festival, he mistook me for you and said he wanted to give you an obi." Naeko spoke pointedly. "That obi maker, that weaver, is really longing for you. I'm something of a woman; I understand that much."

Chieko suppressed her embarrassment.

"Wouldn't you accept it?"

Naeko was silent.

"I told him you were my sister. I'm having him weave it for you."

"I'll accept it, Miss." Naeko bowed her head obediently. "I'm sorry I said what I did."

"He'll deliver it to you. What's the name of your house?"

"Murase," Naeko answered. "It will be a magnificent obi, I'm sure, but someone like me would never have a place to wear it."

"Naeko, no one knows where life's path will take him."

"That's true. That's true," Naeko nodded. "But I don't want to go out in the world. Even if I can't wear it, though, I'll keep it as a treasure."

"Our shop doesn't handle many obis, but I'll find a kimono to go with the one Hideo is making." Chieko continued, "My father's quite a strange fellow. Recently he's had bad feelings about our business. It wouldn't do for a variety wholesale shop like ours to handle only the best items. Lately, we've had more and more synthetics and woolens."

Naeko looked up at the branches of the cedars and stood up from covering Chieko's back.

"A few drops are still falling. You were cramped, weren't you?"

"No . . . I'm thankful."

"What if you were to help out at the shop, Miss?"

"Me?" Chieko stood up as if she had been struck.

Naeko's clothes clung to her skin, soaking wet.

Naeko did not see Chieko all the way to the bus stop—not because she was wet, but because she was afraid of being noticed.

When Chieko returned to the shop, her mother was in the back beyond the entry room preparing snacks for the clerks.

"Mother, I'm sorry I'm so late. Is Father home?"

"He's in behind the curtains you made, thinking about something." Chieko's mother looked at her. "Where have you been? Your clothes are all wet and wrinkled. You should change."

Chieko went upstairs and slowly changed her clothes. She sat for a while, then went downstairs again. Her mother had finished serving the clerks their three o'clock refreshments.

"Mother," Chieko spoke in a wavering voice. "I have something I want to talk about with you, alone."

Shige nodded. "Let's go upstairs in the back."

Chieko's manner became a bit formal. "Was there a thundershower here, too?"

"A thundershower? No. But that's not what you want to talk about, is it?"

"Mother, I went to the Kitayama cedar village. My sister is there. We're twins. I met her for the first time at the Gion Festival this year. She says my real father and mother died long ago."

This naturally took Shige by surprise. She simply looked into Chieko's face. "Kitayama village?"

"I couldn't keep it from you. I've only met her twice . . . at the Gion festival and today."

"What is she doing now?"

"She's apprenticed to a house in the cedar village. She works there. She's a good girl, but she won't come here to our home."

"Hmm." Shige was silent for a moment. "It's good that you should know. What are you going to do?"

"Mother, this is my home. You've made me your child." Her face became intent.

"Of course. You've been my daughter for twenty years."

"Mother." Chieko laid her head on Shige's lap.

"Actually, since the Gion Festival, sometimes—just a little, but sometimes—you've seemed distracted. I thought about asking you if you'd found someone you liked!"

Chieko was silent.

"Why don't you bring the girl here sometime . . . after the clerks have gone home. Maybe in the evening."

Chieko shook her head slightly on Shige's lap. "She won't come. She even calls me 'Miss.'"

"Really?" Shige stroked Chieko's hair. "She must have talked a good deal. Does she look a lot like you?"

The bell crickets in the Tamba jar had begun to chirp.

The Green of Pines

Having heard of a house for sale at a reasonable price near Nanzenji Temple, Takichiro invited his wife and daughter to go with him to see it—in part just for the chance to walk in the fine autumn weather.

"Do you plan to buy it?" Shige asked.

"I'll decide that after I've seen it." He suddenly appeared cross. "The price is good, but it's a small house."

Shige did not respond.

"Let's go even if it's just for the walk. Wouldn't that be all right?"

"Well . . . yes."

Shige felt uneasy. If he were to buy the house, would he commute to their shop? As in Tokyo's Ginza and Nihonbashi, many of the wholesalers in Nakagyo had begun to buy separate homes and commute to their shops. It might not hurt to follow suit. The Sadas' shop, Maruta, was having troubles, but there was probably enough money to spare to buy a small second home.

But wasn't Takichiro planning to sell the shop and "withdraw from the world" in the small house? Or maybe he thought that as long as they had the spare money he should do something daring. But if that were the case, what would Takichiro do living in a small house near Nanzenji Temple? He was in his late fifties. Shige wanted him to live as he liked. The shop would bring a reasonable price, but living off the bank interest would be a rather discouraging life. If the money were invested wisely, they could live comfortably, but Shige could not think of anyone to handle the investment.

Chieko seemed to sense her mother's uneasiness although Shige did not mention it to her. Chieko was young. Solace filled her eyes as she looked at her mother. Takichiro, however, was enjoying himself.

"Father, as long as we'll be walking over that way, could we go a little way into Shoren'in?" Chieko asked in the car. "Just in front of the entrance."

"The camphor trees. That's what you want to see, isn't it?"

"That's right." Chieko was surprised at her father's correct guess. "The camphor trees."

"All right. Let's go," Takichiro said. "I used to sit in the shade of the big camphor trees there and talk with my friends. . . . None of them are in Kyoto anymore."

Chieko was silent.

"That whole area brings back memories."

After leaving her father to his youthful recollections for a moment, Chieko spoke. "I haven't seen those trees in the daylight since I finished school. Father, you know the evening tour bus route? Shoren'in is one of the temples on it. When the bus arrives, several of the priests come out carrying lighted lanterns to meet the guests."

The path along which the guests were led to the vestibule was rather long by the light of the priests' lanterns. But that was about the extent of the artistic effect.

According to the tour bus brochure, the temple nuns were to serve tea to the visitors, but the tourists were actually sent through a tea shop.

"It's all planned in advance to be a big rush. A bunch of people put some rough-looking teacups on a large tray, hurry out, put them down, and scurry back," Chieko said, laughing. "The nuns may have something to do with it, but it must be some amazing sleight of hand; I never caught sight of them! It was quite disillusioning. . . and the tea was just lukewarm."

"That can't be helped. Wouldn't it take a lot of time to do it carefully?" her father said.

"Yes, it would, but it was all right. The garden is illuminated from all sides. A priest comes out in the center and gives a fine talk—just an explanation of the Shoren'in—but he's so eloquent."

Takichiro was silent.

"You can hear the sound of a koto being played somewhere in the temple. My friend and I talked about whether it was the real thing or a recording. Then we went to see the *maiko* at Gion," Chieko continued. "They danced two or three numbers at the Kabuki Renba, but I wonder what sort of *maiko* they were."

"Why is that?"

"Their obis hung loosely, and their clothes looked so shabby."

"Really?"

"From Gion we went to Kadoya at Shimabara to see the grand courtesans. The clothes were all authentic . . . and the young girl attendants', too. In the light of one hundred candles—isn't it called the 'exchanging of cups?'—anyway, they were dressed like that. Then they appeared in traveling costume."

"Well, even that is a lot to see," Takichiro said.

"Yes, the lantern greeting at Shoren'in and Shimabara were fine," Chieko said. "But, it seems as though I've talked about this before."

"Take me with you sometime. I've never seen Kadoya or the grand courtesans." They arrived in front of Shoren'in just as her mother spoke.

Why did Chieko want to see the camphor trees? Was it because she had walked among the rows of camphor trees at the Botanical Garden? Was it because she said that she preferred the trees of nature to the Kitayama cedars, which were grown as a crop?

Four camphor trees stood in a row above the rock wall at the entrance to Shoren'in. The nearer ones seemed to be very old.

Chieko and her parents stood silently looking at the camphor trees. They could sense the weird power of the giant trees in the uncanny way that the branches spread out and joined together.

"Well, shall we go?" Takichiro started walking toward Nanzenji Temple.

Takichiro spoke as he examined the directions to the house, which were written on a paper he had taken from his wallet. "Chieko, I don't know much about them, but don't camphor trees grow in warm climates? Aren't they southern trees? Don't they flourish in places like Atami or Kyushu? These are old trees, but don't you think they look like oversized bonsai?"

"Isn't that the way it is with Kyoto? Isn't it the same with the mountains and rivers . . . and the people, too?" Chieko said.

"Maybe so," her father nodded. "But not all people. That's not always true with people."

Chieko did not respond.

"Whether it's people today or people from ancient history."

"I see."

"If we put it your way, Chieko, wouldn't that be true for all of Japan?"

Chieko marveled at how far her father had taken her comment.

"Father, if you look closely at the trunks of those trees and the strangely spreading limbs, don't they seem frightening, as though they possess some great power?"

"They do, but does a young girl like you think of such things?" Her father looked back at the trees. Then he stared at his daughter. "Certainly, it's as you say . . . and even in the way your lustrous hair has grown . . . but your old father has become rather dull. Maybe I've grown quite decrepit."

"Father," Chieko called out, her voice filled with intense compassion.

Although the precincts of the temple were quite spacious and quiet, there were, as always, few signs of people inside the main gate of Nanzenji Temple. Takichiro turned left as he studied the map to the house. It was quite a small house, but it was situated far back from the street, and the earthen wall around it was high. White bush clover bloomed in long stretches on both sides of the walk from the narrow gate to the door.

"Look, how lovely." Takichiro stood motionless in front of the gate, fascinated by the beauty of the white bush clover. But he had already lost the desire to examine the house to buy it; he noticed that a large home two doors away had been converted into an inn.

Still, something about the clover made it difficult to leave.

In the years since Takichiro had last visited Nanzenji, many of the houses on the street nearby had been converted to inns, and this took him by surprise. The houses had been rebuilt inside to accommodate large groups. Students from the country, visiting Kyoto on school excursions, caused a great commotion going in and out.

"The house itself is all right, but this just won't do," Takichiro whispered as he stood at the gate. "I wonder if time will turn all of Kyoto into nothing but inns . . . just like the area around Kodaiji Temple. The strip between Kyoto and Osaka has become an industrial zone. There is still some open land around Nishinokyo, but even if you could put up with the inconvenience of living that far away, who knows what sort of fancy, high-collar houses they might build in that neighborhood." Takichiro's discouragement showed in his face.

Takichiro still seemed to feel an attachment to the rows of white bush clover. He walked seven or eight steps away, then, alone, he turned and looked at them again. Shige and Chieko stood waiting for him in the street.

"The man who owns this house got them to bloom so well." He returned to where Chieko and her mother were standing together. "I wonder what his secret is. He probably should have used some bamboo supports for the clover. When it rains, you can't walk on the flagstones without getting all wet from the leaves," Takichiro said. "He probably didn't have a mind to sell the house when he tried to get the clover to bloom this year, but once he had to sell it, he didn't care whether it got bent or tangled."

Chieko and her mother said nothing.

"I wonder if man is just that way." Takichiro frowned a bit.

"Father, do you like clover that much?" Chieko said, trying to brighten the moment. "It's too late this year, but I'll design a bush clover print for you for next year."

"Clover would be a woman's pattern. No, clover would be for a woman's summer kimono."

"I'd try to make something that wouldn't look as though it were for a woman."

"Well, what would you use a clover print for? . . . under-wear?" Takichiro looked at his daughter. His thoughts diverted with laughter, he said, "And for your kindness I'll make you a kimono or a jacket in a camphor tree pattern. It would look like a design for a ghost. It would be as though women and men were turned around backwards."

"No, it wouldn't."

"Would you go out wearing some ghostly camphor tree pattern?"

"Yes, I would. Anywhere."

"Hmm." Her father looked down. He seemed to be deep in thought. "Chieko, it's not that I dislike the white bush clover. Some flowers touch me depending on the time and place that I see them."

"I suppose so . . . ," Chieko answered. "Father, since we've come this far and Tatsumura's is close by, I'd like to drop in."

"Oh, that store for foreigners. What shall we do, Shige?"

"If Chieko wants to go . . . ," she answered lightheartedly.

"Well, Tatsumura's obis don't appear in the stores."

The shop was in a neighborhood of fine old homes in lower Kawaramachi.

Entering the store, Chieko began to look at the silk fabric for women, which was stacked in rows along the right side. They were not Tatsumura's own designs, but weaves from the Kanebo company.

Shige approached her daughter. "Are you planning to wear Western-style clothes?"

"No, Mother. I was just wondering what kind of silk foreigners prefer."

Her mother nodded. She stood behind her daughter, occasionally putting out her hand to touch the silk.

In the middle room and in the hall hung prints of Shosoin cloth and ancient fabrics.

This was Tatsumura's work. Takichiro had seen Tatsumura's displays many times, and he had often seen the original classic fabrics and patterns. He knew them all by name and by sight, but he could not help but examine these closely.

"These are to show the foreigners that we can make such things in Japan," a clerk said. Takichiro recognized his face.

Takichiro had heard the same thing when he visited the shop previously, but he nodded again this time. "Ancient times were amazing . . . over a thousand years ago . . . ," he said in regard to the reproductions of Tang Chinese fabrics.

They did not seem to sell large pieces of cloth in the old prints. Takichiro liked such fabric and had bought several obis made from it for Shige and Chieko, but this shop was oriented toward foreigners and did not seem to have obis. The biggest thing they sold seemed to be table runners.

Small articles, such as bags, paper holders, cigarette cases, and crepe wrappers, were decoratively arranged in ornamental boxes.

Takichiro bought two or three Tatsumura neckties that did not look like Tatsumura's work, and also a Kikumomi paper holder. Kikumomi was a reproduction in cloth of a craft called Daikikumomi, which had been made in Takagatake by Koetsu over three hundred years ago.

"Where was it in Tohoku? There's a place where they still make something that looks like this out of strong Japanese paper," Takichiro said.

"Yes, yes," the clerk replied. "But I don't know much about the connection with Koetsu."

There were portable Sony radios lined up on top of the ornamental boxes in the back, which naturally surprised Takichiro and his wife and daughter, even if they were merely consignment goods for the purpose of acquiring foreign currency.

The three of them were led to a receiving room in the rear, where they were served tea. The clerk told them that many so-called noble visitors from foreign countries had once sat in the chairs where they were now seated.

Outside the window was a small, but unusual, grove of cedar trees.

"What kind of cedar is that?" Takichiro asked.

"I'm not sure, but I think it's called a *koyo* cedar or something like that."

"What Chinese character do you use to write '*koyo*'?"

"The gardener doesn't always know how to write the names, but wouldn't it be the characters for 'broad leaf'? Whatever it is, they grow from Honshu on toward the south."

"What makes the trunk that color?"

"That's moss."

They turned around at the sound of a portable radio starting to play and saw a young man explaining something to three or four Western women.

"That's Shin'ichi's older brother." Chieko stood up.

Shin'ichi's brother Ryusuke stepped toward Chieko. He bowed his head to her parents in the receiving room.

"Are you acting as a guide for those ladies?" Chieko asked. As Chieko and Ryusuke approached each other, she found it difficult to speak to this young man, so different from the easygoing Shin'ichi. She felt ill at ease.

"Not as a guide. A friend of mine was going around with them as an interpreter, but his younger sister died, so I'm taking his place for a few days."

"What? His younger sister?"

"Yes, she was about two years younger than Shin'ichi. She was a cute girl."

Chieko did not speak.

"Shin'ichi's English isn't very good. He's shy. And, well, I . . . we don't need anything like an interpreter here at the shop. These are the kind of customers who buy portable radios. They're American women staying at the Miyako Hotel."

"I see."

"The hotel is close by, so we dropped in here. I wish they would look at our fabrics, but no . . . it's radios," Ryusuke laughed in a whisper. "I suppose it's all right either way."

"This is the first time I've seen radios for sale at a place like this."

"Portable radios or silks—a dollar is a dollar. It's all the same."

"I see."

"Just a moment ago we went out into the garden. There are a number of different colors of carp in the pond. I was wondering how I could explain the carp if they ask me details about them. All I could think of was 'beautiful, beautiful.' I was certainly glad to find you here and get away from them. I don't know anything about carp. I wouldn't know what to say in English about the colors. 'Some have spots . . .'" Ryusuke paused a moment. "Chieko, shall we go out and look at the carp?"

"What about the ladies?"

"It would be better to leave them with the clerk, here. They'll be going back to the hotel for tea soon. They're supposed to meet their husbands there to go to Nara."

"I'll tell my father and mother."

"I'll have to go talk to the ladies, too, and excuse myself." Ryusuke went to the women and said something. The ladies all looked toward Chieko at the same time. Chieko blushed.

Ryusuke returned immediately and led Chieko into the garden.

The two of them sat down by the pond and watched the splendidly colored carp swimming about. Chieko and Ryusuke were silent for a moment.

"Chieko, the clerk at your shop—since your business is incorporated now I don't know if you call him the manager or director—I think you need to approach him rather forcefully and ask him some questions. You could, couldn't you? I'd go with you if you'd like."

Chieko had not expected to hear anything like this. Her heart shrank.

The night after she returned from Tatsumura's shop Chieko had a dream. Schools of various kinds of carp gathered at her feet as she knelt at the edge of the pond. The carp piled one on top of another, dancing as they stuck their heads out above the surface of the water.

That was all there was to the dream. It was as it was in the afternoon. The fish drew closer when Chieko put her hand in the water and made ripples on the surface of the pond. She was startled, but she felt an inexpressible affection for the carp.

Ryusuke, who was standing at Chieko's side, was even more surprised.

"What kind of fragrance . . . what kind spirit emanates from your hand?" Ryusuke said.

Embarrassed at these words, Chieko stood up. "The carp are probably accustomed to people."

Ryusuke stared at Chieko's profile.

"Higashiyama is right over there," Chieko said, avoiding Ryusuke's eyes.

"Don't the colors look a bit different? . . . more like autumn?" Ryusuke asked.

After awakening, Chieko could not quite recall whether Ryusuke had been at her side in the carp dream. For a while she could not sleep.

The next day Chieko hesitated to say that Ryusuke had encouraged her to confront the clerk.

As closing time approached, Chieko sat down in front of the account register. It was in an old-fashioned booth surrounded by low lattice work. Uemura, the head clerk, noticed Chieko's uncommonly serious air. "Miss Chieko, what do you need?"

"Would you please show me some of our kimono fabric?"

"Ours?" Uemura seemed relieved. "You're going to wear a kimono from our shop? If you want one now, then is it for New Year's? A visiting kimono or a long-sleeved one? Let's see, aren't you going to buy yours at a dye shop like Okazaki or a place like Eriman?"

"I want you to show me some of our *Yuzen*. It's not for New Year's."

"I would show you all we have, but I wonder if there's anything that would suit the tastes of a girl with a practiced eye like yours." Uemura stood up, called two clerks, and whispered to them. Together the three of them took out ten bolts of cloth and unrolled them in the middle of the floor, arranging them with an experienced hand.

"This one will be fine." Chieko chose quickly. "Could you have it done in five days or a week? I'll leave the details up to you . . . the lining color and such."

Uemura was taken aback. "It's quite sudden. We're a wholesale shop, so we seldom send things out to be made, but it's all right."

The two clerks deftly rolled up the fabric.

"Here are the measurements." Chieko placed a paper on Uemura's desk, but did not turn to leave. "Mr. Uemura, I'd like to learn about the business here a little at a time. I hope you'll help me," Chieko spoke in a gentle voice, bowing her head slightly.

"Certainly." Uemura's face stiffened.

Chieko spoke quietly, "Tomorrow would be all right, but would you show me the account ledger, too?"

"The account ledger?" Uemura seemed to smile bitterly. "Are you going to study the accounts?"

"Nothing so ambitious as that. I thought I would just take a glance at it. I don't know anything about the business, you know."

"Yes, the account ledger involves quite a lot. I couldn't explain it all in one sitting. There are also things like taxes and such."

"Does our shop use a double ledger?"

"What do you mean? I'd certainly be asking for your help if you could do a trick like that. Ours is all on the up and up."

"Please show it to me tomorrow, Mr. Uemura," Chieko said bluntly and stepped away.

"I've taken care of this shop since before you were born, Miss Chieko," Uemura said, but she would not turn back. "What does she mean . . . ," Uemura spoke inaudibly. Then he smacked his tongue. "My back hurts."

When Chieko returned to where her mother was preparing supper, Shige seemed completely astonished. "Chieko, you said some rather forceful things."

"It wasn't easy."

"Young people can be alarming, even when they seem gentle. I was almost shaking just listening to you."

"I got the idea from someone else."

"Really? Who?"

"Shin'ichi's older brother, at Tatsumura's. Their father is still doing well in business. He said they have two good clerks, so if Mr. Uemura were to quit, he would send one of them here or he'd come himself."

"You mean Ryusuke?"

"Yes, he's going into business anyway so he can quit graduate school anytime."

"Really?" Shige looked at her daughter's lovely beaming face. "But Mr. Uemura doesn't show any signs of planning to quit."

"And he said if a good house turned up over near the white clover house, he'd have his father buy it."

"I see." Shige could say nothing else for the moment. "Your father *has* grown weary of the world."

"He said, 'Wouldn't that be good for your father?' "

"Ryusuke said that?"

"Yes. Oh, and Mother, you probably heard me mention it to the clerk, but I'm going to send one of our kimonos to the girl in the cedar village. Is that all right?"

"Of course. And how about a jacket to go with it?"

Chieko looked away, her eyes filling with tears.

Why were they called "high looms"? Of course, the looms themselves were tall. The earth was hollowed out slightly beneath them so they rested low in the ground. Some said this was because the dampness of the earth was good for the thread. Originally, a person sometimes sat on top of the loom, but now they put heavy stones in baskets and suspended them from the sides.

Some weaving houses used both hand looms and machine looms.

At Hideo's shop they had three hand looms at which the three brothers wove. Since their father, Sosuke, also worked at the loom occasionally, their shop fared well among the numerous small hand-weaving businesses in Nishijin.

Hideo's joy increased as the obi that Chieko had requested neared completion. Perhaps it was because he was finishing a work into which he had put his whole heart or because he could perceive Chieko in the movement of the reeds of the loom and the sounds of the weaving.

No, it was not Chieko. It was Naeko. The obi was not Chieko's obi, but Naeko's. Nevertheless, as Hideo wove, Chieko and Naeko became one.

Hideo's father, Sosuke, stood beside him for a moment, watching. "My, that's a beautiful obi. And what an unusual pattern." He inclined his head. "Whose is it?"

"It's for Sada's daughter, Chieko."

"And the pattern?"

"Chieko designed it."

"Really. Chieko did? Hmm." Sosuki seemed to swallow his breath. He gazed at the obi still on the loom, touching it with his fingers. "Hideo, your weaving is precise. That's good." Sosuke hesitated. "Hideo, I think I talked about this before, but I feel I'm indebted to Mr. Sada."

"I know, Father."

"I suppose I have already told you," he said, but he continued all the same. "It was half on borrowed money that I was able to get my first loom and start in the weaving business on my own. Every time I wove an obi I used to deliver it to Mr. Sada. It was so embarrassing to take a single obi to him that I always went quietly at night."

Hideo was silent.

"Mr. Sada never looked displeased. Now we have three looms, and somehow or another, well . . . we manage. Even so, our social position is different . . . ."

"I know, but why are you talking about such things?"

"You seem to be quite fond of Chieko."

"Is that what it is?" Hideo had been resting, but he put his hands and feet back to the loom and continued weaving.

As soon as the obi was finished, Hideo quickly left for Naeko's cedar village to deliver it.

It was afternoon. A rainbow had appeared several times in the direction of Kitayama.

Hideo noticed the rainbow as he stepped into the road carrying Naeko's obi under his arm. The rainbow was wide, but the colors were pale, and the upper portion of the arc was missing. Hideo stopped, and, as he watched, the colors turned faint as if they would vanish.

Before the bus entered the mountains, Hideo saw the same kind of rainbow twice more. None of the rainbows were perfectly shaped to the top; they all had thin spots. It was not an uncommon sort of rainbow, but today Hideo was somewhat concerned. Were these rainbows a sign of good luck or bad?

The sky was not cloudy, but after he entered the forest he could not tell if yet another rainbow appeared because of the mountains that pressed in on the banks of the Kiyotaki River.

Hideo got off the bus at the Kitayama village. Naeko, wearing her work clothes and wiping her wet hands on her apron, walked up to him immediately.

She had been carefully washing a log with Bodai sand. It was still only October, but the mountain water was probably cold. The log was floating in a man-made trough. Hot water seemed to be running from a simple kettle on one side where steam was rising.

"Oh, thank you for coming such a long way back here in the mountains." Naeko bowed deeply.

"This is the obi you were promised. I came to deliver it."

"It's the obi I'm to receive in Chieko's place. I don't like being her substitute. I was happy enough just to meet her," Naeko said.

"This obi was promised to you, wasn't it? And it's even Chieko's own design."

Naeko looked down. "The day before yesterday, Hideo, I received everything to go with the obi, from kimono to sandals . . . all from Chieko's shop. Where could I ever wear things like that?"

"What about the Festival of Ages on the twenty-second? Couldn't you get away then?"

"Yes, I could," Naeko answered without hesitation. "People will see us here." She seemed to be thinking. "Let's go to the riverbed, by those flat rocks."

It would not be appropriate for them to hide among the cedars as she had done with Chieko the previous time.

"This obi you made will be the treasure of my life."

"Oh, no. I'll make one for you again."

Naeko could not speak.

The family who looked after Naeko knew, of course, that Chieko had sent the kimono, so it would have been no problem for Naeko to have taken Hideo to the house. But since Naeko generally understood Chieko's circumstances now and knew about the shop, that alone was enough to satisfy the desire she had cherished since childhood to find her sister. Besides, she did not want to cause trouble for Chieko.

Indeed, since the Murase family, who had raised Naeko and for whom she now worked so ungrudgingly, were landholders in the cedar mountains, it could not cause any problems for Chieko's family if the truth were to be revealed. It may be that a landholder in the cedar mountains is in a more stable position than a middle-class dry goods wholesaler.

So, although Chieko's affection had naturally touched Naeko's heart, Naeko intended to avoid seeing Chieko further and deepening their acquaintance.

Naeko led Hideo to some flat stones in the plain of the Kiyotaki River. Even in the river bottom, as many cedars as would fit were planted among the small stones.

"I'm sorry I was so rude," Naeko said. She was a young girl and wanted to see the obi as soon as possible.

"The cedar mountains are beautiful," Hideo said, looking up as he untied the cotton cloth around the bundle and loosened the string around the wrapping paper. "This is where the bow would be and this is supposed to be the front."

"Oh." Naeko stroked the obi. "It's too good for me." Her eyes brightened.

"What could be too good about an obi woven by some young fellow like me? When I heard it was to be cedars and red pines, I thought since it's close to New Year's the bow should be pines, but Chieko said it should be cedars. Now that I've come here I realize why. When you think of cedars, you think of stands of old trees, but, drawn gently, they have their merit. There are also some trunks of red pines, for color harmony."

Of course the color of the cedar trunks was not reproduced exactly in the obi. There was a style in the color and design.

"It's a splendid obi. Thank you so much. But a person like me can't wear a showy obi like this one."

"Does it go well with the kimono Chieko sent?"

"I think they'll go together very well."

"Chieko has been well acquainted with the kimono styles in

Kyoto since she was little. I haven't shown her this obi. Somehow I feel embarrassed to."

"But it's her own design. I want her to see it."

"You'll wear it to the Festival of Ages, won't you?" Hideo said, as he folded the obi and placed it inside the wrapping paper.

When he finished tying the string Hideo spoke to Naeko, "Please accept this willingly. I was the one who promised the obi, but Chieko asked me to make it. Please think of me only as the weaver. . . . But I *did* put my heart into weaving it for you."

Hideo placed the obi on her knees. Naeko was silent.

"Chieko has seen kimonos all her life. She is familiar with styles, so I'm certain it will go with the kimono she sent you . . . as I mentioned before."

The flow in the shallows of the Kiyotaki River in front of the two of them made a tiny, delicate sound. Hideo looked around at the cedars on both sides of the banks. "I realized that the trunks of the trees would probably stand uniformly side by side like crafted pieces, but even the leaves on the upper branches look like flowers, though rather plain and somber ones."

Naeko's face wore a touch of sorrow. Her father had worked as a branch cutter. Surely he had fallen as he jumped from branch to branch. Had he been pained in his heart for the child he had abandoned—Chieko? At that time Naeko, too, had been a baby; she could not have known anything. The people of the village had told her after she was older.

If it were possible, Naeko had wanted to see her sister, even if it were only a single, casual glimpse.

Naeko's original home still stood abandoned in the cedar village, weathered and dilapidated, since she could not live there alone. For a long time she had lived with a middle-aged couple who worked in the cedar mountains and their daughter who attended primary school. Naturally she paid no rent; they were not the sort of people who would accept it.

The primary school girl was strangely fond of flowers. There was a single fragrant golden olive tree at the house. The girl would occasionally come to ask "Big Sister Naeko" to help prune the tree.

"Just leave it alone and it will be fine," Naeko answered. As they passed the house, Naeko was able to perceive the fragrance of the olive blossoms from a greater distance than most people. That was to Naeko rather a sad discovery.

When Naeko placed the obi on her lap, her legs began to feel heavy. Thoughts filled her mind.

"Now that I know where Chieko is, I don't want to continue to see her. I'll wear the kimono and obi just this once. You understand, don't you?" Naeko spoke from her heart.

"Yes," Hideo said. "Please come to the Festival of Ages. I'd like to have Chieko see you wearing the kimono and obi, but I won't invite her. The festival parade begins at Gosho, so I'll wait for you at the Hamaguri Gate on the west side. Is that all right?"

Naeko's cheeks blushed lightly for a moment, then she nodded deeply.

A small tree stood at the water's edge on the far side; the reflection of its crimson leaves shivered in the flow of the river. Hideo looked up. "What kind of tree is that turning such a bright red?"

"That's a lacquer tree," Naeko said, lifting her eyes. As she answered, she gathered her hair with her shaking hand, but somehow it came undone and cascaded down her back.

"Oh."

Naeko blushed. She tried to pull her hair back up and twist it, holding the hairpin in her mouth. She stuck the pin in her hair, but this pin, which had once let her hair loose, seemed insufficient to hold it now.

Hideo admired the hair and Naeko's beautiful movements.

"You let your hair grow long," he said.

"Yes. Chieko doesn't cut hers either. She does it up so well a man wouldn't know." Naeko hurriedly put a towel on her head. "Excuse me."

Hideo did not respond.

"Here it's as if I do makeup for the cedars when I polish the logs, but I don't use any myself."

Even so, it appeared as if she wore the faintest trace of lipstick. Hideo wished she would take off the towel once more and let him see her hair down her back again, but he could not bring himself to ask.

The mountain on the west side of the narrow valley began to turn slightly dark.

"Naeko, I suppose you have to be going." Hideo stood up.

"The days are getting shorter. Work is almost finished for today."

Hideo looked at the golden colors of the sunset between the straight rows of the trunks of the trees on the summit of the mountain east of the valley.

"Hideo, thank you. Thank you very much." Naeko stood up, accepting the obi with a delicate movement.

"If you thank anyone, you should thank Chieko," Hideo said, but the joy of having woven an obi for this daughter of the cedar mountains swelled warm within him. "I may sound persistent, but be sure to be at the west gate at Gosho, the Hamaguri Gate."

"I will," Naeko nodded deeply. "I'll feel awkward in an obi and kimono I've never worn before, but . . ."

The Festival of the Ages on October twenty-second along with the Aoi Festival of the Kamigamo and Shimogamo Shrines and the Gion Festival were called the "three great festivals" of the old capital. The Festival of Ages was a celebration of the Heian Shrine, but the procession began at Kyoto's Gosho.

From early morning Naeko had been unable to calm herself. Now she had been waiting for Hideo in the shadow of Hamaguri Gate since half an hour before the appointed time. This was the first time she had waited for a man.

Fortunately, the sky was clear and blue.

Heian Shrine was built in 1895, the twenty-eighth year of the Meiji Period, one thousand years after the removal of the capital from Nara to Kyoto, so naturally the Festival of Ages was the newest of the "three great festivals." Since the procession commemorated the inauguration of Kyoto as the capital, one thousand years of changes in customs were displayed in the parade, each era being represented in costumes worn by a person portraying a famous personality associated with the time.

For example, there was the Empress Kazunomiya, the poetess Rengetsu, and the grand courtesan Yoshino. There were also Izumo no Okuni, the legendary founder of Kabuki, and Hideyoshi's concubine Yodogimi. Lady Tokiwa, Yokobue, and Lady Tomoe also appeared, as well as Lady Shizuka, Ono no Komachi, Murasaki Shikibu, and Sei Shonagon.

Then there were the Ohara women and the Katsura women. These women and others, courtesans, female performers, and women venders, were scattered throughout the processions. Naturally there were men like Kusunoki Masashige, Oda Nobunaga, Toyotomi Hideyoshi, imperial court noblemen, and warriors.

This procession was like a long scroll of Kyoto customs unrolling before the viewers.

Women had been added to the procession in 1950, making it ever so much more showy and beautiful.

Leading the procession were Loyalists of the time of the Meiji Restoration and the mountain troops of Kitakuwada in Tamba. In the rear were the civil officials of the Enryaku Period in line for an imperial visit. When the procession made its way back to Gosho, Shinto prayers were recited before the imperial carriage.

The procession left from Gosho and could be seen well from the plaza at Gosho. That's why Hideo invited Naeko to this spot.

Although crowds of people were going in and out, no one seemed to notice Naeko waiting for Hideo in the shade of the gate. Finally one lady, who seemed to be the wife of a shop owner, came straight toward Naeko. "Miss, what a beautiful obi! Where did you buy it? It looks so good with your outfit." She started to touch it. "Would you show me the bow in the back?"

Naeko turned around. Surprisingly, being watched by the woman made her feel at ease.

Hideo arrived. "Thank you for waiting."

All the seats next to Gosho, from which the parade would leave, were taken by travel clubs and shrine societies, but Hideo and Naeko stood behind the tourists' seats.

This was the first time Naeko had seen the parade from such a good spot. She watched the procession, quite forgetful of her new clothes and of Hideo.

Noticing that Hideo was not watching the procession, Naeko asked, "Hideo, what are you looking at?"

"The green of the pines . . . and the parade. The pines in the background make the parade look all the better. The expansive gardens here in Gosho are mostly black pines. They're my favorite . . . and I've also been looking at you out of the corner of my eye. You didn't notice, did you?"

Naeko cast her eyes down.

Deep Autumn Sisters

Of all the festivals of Kyoto, Chieko enjoyed the Kurama Fire Festival even more than the Daimonji. Naeko had also gone to it; the festival was not very far from her home. But, if they had once passed each other there, neither of them had ever noticed.

Partitions of tree branches were constructed at the houses along the path from Kurama Road to the shrine, and water was poured on the roofs. In the middle of the night, people decorated their homes with all kinds of torches, large and small.

Chanting "sareya, sareyo," participants climbed the hill toward the shrine. The flames burned fiercely. Then, when the palanquin appeared, the village women all came out to pull it with ropes. Toward the end of the festival, an offering was made of a great torch. The celebration continued almost until daylight.

But this year the Fire Festival had been cancelled. Some said it was for financial reasons. The Bamboo Cutting Festival, however, was held as usual.

The Taro Festival of Kitano Tenjin Shrine was also cancelled this year. Some said it was because the poor taro harvest prevented their making a taro palanquin.

In Kyoto, there were many events like the Pumpkin Service at Anrakuyoji Temple at Shishigatani and the Imperial Offering of Cucumbers at Rengeji Temple. Might this reveal an aspect of both the old capital and its people?

Among the recently revived traditions were the dragon-headed Karyobinga boats on the Arashiyama River and the feast held on the banks of the meandering stream in the garden of Kamigamo Shrine. Both were originally the elegant diversions of the nobility. At the stream feast, participants sat on the bank, dressed in old costumes, composing poetry and drawing pictures. As the wine cup came floating down the stream before them, they took it up and drank from it. Then, assisted by young boys, they sent it on downstream to the next person.

The event had started the previous year. Chieko had gone to see it. The leader of the noble families had been the Japanese traditional poet, Yoshii Isamu, who has since passed away.

The traditional event, having been newly revived after years of neglect, was somehow not very inviting.

Chieko had not seen the Karyobinga at Arashiyama this year, either. She was inclined to think that it was unlikely that the event would have any of the rustic elegance of old. In Kyoto, there were more ancient festivals than one could possibly see.

Was it because she was raised by her hardworking mother, or was Chieko naturally of such a character that she arose early to polish the lattice work?

"Chieko, you two seemed to be having a good time at the Festival of Ages." After she finished cleaning up for breakfast, she received a telephone call from Shin'ichi. It seemed he, too, had mistaken Naeko for Chieko.

"You were there? You should have said something." Chieko shrugged her shoulders.

"I started to, but my brother stopped me," Shin'ichi said effortlessly.

Chieko hesitated to tell him it was a case of mistaken identity. Chieko learned from Shin'ichi that Naeko had been wearing Hideo's obi at the Festival of Ages as well as the kimono she had sent, and that the person accompanying Naeko had surely been Hideo. That news took Chieko by surprise, but soon she felt a faint warmth in her heart as a smile came to her lips.

"Chieko, Chieko," Shin'ichi called her name over the telephone. "Why aren't you saying anything?"

"Aren't you the one who called me?"

"That's right," Shin'ichi laughed. "Are the clerks there now?"

"No. Not yet."

"Chieko, do you have a cold?"

"Do I sound as though I do? I was just out front cleaning the lattice door."

"I see." It sounded as though Shin'ichi was shaking the receiver.

This time Chieko laughed.

Shin'ichi spoke in low tones. "Actually, I'm calling for my brother. Here he is."

Chieko could not speak to Ryusuke in so carefree a manner as to Shin'ichi.

"Chieko, did you talk to the clerk?"

"Yes."

"Great." Ryusuke spoke in a powerful voice. "Great."

"My mother caught wind of it, so she's been a little uneasy."

"I would imagine."

"I told him I want him to show me the account ledger because I'd like to learn the family business."

"That's good. Just talking to him changed his attitude, didn't it?"

"Then I had him get the bank books, stocks, and such out of the safe."

"That's excellent, Chieko. You did well . . . ," but Ryusuke could not resist his emotions, "for such a gentle girl."

"It was your idea."

"It wasn't my idea. There's been a rumor among the wholesalers in the neighborhood. If you hadn't said anything to him, we had decided that either my father or I should go, but it was better for you to do it. The clerk's attitude changed, didn't it?"

"Yes, somewhat."

"I thought so." Ryusuke was silent for a long while. "That's good."

Chieko sensed that Ryusuke was hesitating.

"Chieko, would I be in the way if I dropped by your shop this afternoon," he asked, "with Shin'ichi?"

"In the way? Of course not," Chieko answered.

"Well, you *are* a young girl."

"Oh, stop it."

"How about it?" Ryusuke laughed. "Would it be all right if I came by while the clerk is still there? I'll take a look for myself. You don't have anything to worry about. I just want to take a look at his face."

"Oh?" The rest of her words would not come out.

Ryusuke's father owned a large wholesale business near Muromachi, and he had many influential friends. Ryusuke was in graduate school, but he was still concerned about the business.

"Then later on we can go have some turtle soup. I'm reserving seats at Oichi in Kitano. Would you come with me? It wouldn't be polite for me to ask your father and mother to go, too, so I'm inviting just you. I'll bring along the festival boy."

Chieko was overawed. All she could say was yes.

It had been more than ten years since Shin'ichi had ridden on the shrine palanquin in the Gion Festival, but his older brother, Ryusuke, still called him "the festival boy," half in ridicule, but also because Shin'ichi was still gentle and lovely like a festival child.

"Ryusuke and Shin'ichi called to say they'll be coming this afternoon," Chieko told her mother.

"What?" Shige, too, seemed surprised.

In the afternoon, Chieko went to the rear of the second floor and carefully put on her makeup, but nothing that would stand out.

Although she tried to do up her long hair she could not suit herself. She tried this and that, wondering what to wear.

When she finally came down, her father was not home. He had gone out.

Chieko prepared the charcoal fire in the parlor, then looked about at the small garden. The moss on the maple tree was still green, but the leaves of the violets had turned slightly yellow. The sasanqua bush at the base of the Christian lantern had put forth its scarlet flowers, and its vivid color touched Chieko's heart more than that of a red rose.

Ryusuke and Shin'ichi greeted Chieko's mother politely when they arrived. Then Ryusuke seated himself squarely in front of the clerk at the register. The clerk Uemura hurriedly came out of the accountant's booth and took quite a long time greeting them all over again. But Ryusuke's sullen face never flickered as he returned the clerk's greeting. Uemura, of course, perceived his coldness.

Uemura wondered what this impudent student was up to. Although he felt oppressed by Ryusuke, there was nothing he could do about it.

Ryusuke waited for a break in Uemura's words. "It's wonderful that the shop is doing well."

"Thank you."

"My father and his associates say it's because Mr. Sada has you here. Your many years of experience are indispensable."

"What do you mean? This isn't a big shop like yours. We're not even worth talking about."

"No, all we've done is expand into different areas. A Kyoto dry goods shop, or whatever we're called—we're really just a big dime store. I don't like it. Why . . . if shops run by solid, reliable people like you were to disappear . . ."

Ryusuke stood up just as Uemura was about to respond. The clerk frowned as he watched the retreating figure of Ryusuke going to the parlor in the rear where Chieko and Shin'ichi were sitting. It was obvious to Uemura that there was some sort of secret connection between Chieko, who had wanted to see the account book, and Ryusuke.

Chieko looked up at Ryusuke's face as if to question him.

"I drove the nail in him. I *am* responsible for advising you as I did."

Chieko did not speak. She looked down as she made some tea for Ryusuke.

"Ryusuke, look at the violets on the maple trunk." Shin'ichi pointed to them. "See, there are two plants. Some years ago Chieko said that the two violets were like two lovers. Though they are close to one another, they've never met."

"Yes."

"Girls think of such cute things."

"Stop it. Aren't you ashamed, Shin'ichi?" Chieko's hand shook slightly as she placed the teacup in front of the older brother.

The three of them went to Oichi, a turtle soup shop at Kitano Rokuban, in Ryusuke's shop car. Oichi was an old shop, well known among tourists. The rooms were old-fashioned with low ceilings.

They had turtle that had been boiled in a so-called round pot and made into a stew.

Chieko felt a warmth swell within her as though she were drunk. A faint peach blush appeared at her neck. It was a beautiful sight to see the color rise in her youthful, white skin, so smooth and delicately grained. A fascinating charm showed in her eyes. Occasionally, she stroked her cheek.

Chieko had never before put so much as a drop of liquor to her lips, but the broth of the stew was almost half sake.

The car was waiting out front, but Chieko was afraid her legs would not hold her; nevertheless, she was cheerful. She felt as though she might speak more freely than usual.

"Shin'ichi," Chieko spoke to the more approachable brother. "The person you saw at the Festival of Ages at the garden of Gosho wasn't me. You were mistaken. She was some distance away, wasn't she?"

"You don't have to hide anything," Shin'ichi laughed.

"I'm not hiding anything . . . " Chieko did not know what to say. "Actually, that was my sister."

"What?" Shin'ichi was dubious.

When the cherries were in bloom at Kiyomizu, Chieko had told Shin'ichi that she was an abandoned child, and surely her confession had made its way to his brother Ryusuke. Even if Shin'ichi had not mentioned it to him, he might well have heard the rumor since their shops were close together.

"The girl you saw at the garden at Gosho was . . . ," Chieko hesitated slightly. "We're twins. . . . She's my sister."

This was the first Shin'ichi had heard of it. He did not respond.

The three were silent for a moment.

"I was the one who was abandoned."

Then Ryusuke spoke. "If that's true, I wish Chieko had been abandoned in front of our shop. Yes, I wish she had been abandoned at our shop," he repeated.

"Ryusuke," Shin'ichi laughed, "it wasn't the Chieko you see now. She was a newborn baby."

"What's wrong with that?" Ryusuke said.

"You're saying that as you look at Chieko now."

"No, I'm not."

"The Chieko you see now is the Chieko that the Sadas have nurtured and loved and raised," Shin'ichi said. "You were still a child then yourself. Could a little child have raised a baby?"

"Yes," Ryusuke answered firmly.

"Hmm. That's your same stubborn confidence. You hate to lose."

"Maybe so, but I would have liked to have taken care of Chieko as a baby. Mother surely would have helped."

Chieko's head cleared. Her forehead turned white.

The autumn festival of the Kitano Dance lasted for two weeks. The day before it ended, Sada Takichiro went there alone.

Naturally, he had received more than one admission ticket from the teahouse, but he did not feel like inviting anyone along. He felt it would be tiresome to go to the teahouse with friends on the way back.

Before the dance festivities, Takichiro gloomily went up to the teahouse. He was unfamiliar with the geisha whose turn it was to perform the tea ceremony.

Seven or eight young girls stood in a line to the side, helping with utensils. Except for one girl in the center in light blue, they all wore matching long-sleeved kimonos in pale pink—the color of the crested ibis.

Takichiro almost called out loud. She was now in makeup, but wasn't this the same girl who had ridden on the streetcar with the mistress from the gay quarters? Perhaps the blue kimono meant it was her turn at something.

The girl in the blue kimono brought some tea and placed it before Takichiro. Of course, she was very prim and did not smile, all according to correct manners.

But Takichiro felt his heart lighten. The dance was "Portrait of Lady Yu Poppies," a dance drama in eight scenes from the well-known tragic Chinese story of Lady Yu and Hsiang Yu.

Lady Yu stabs herself in the chest and dies in the arms of Hsiang Yu, while listening to one of the nostalgic "Songs of Ch'u." Later, after Hsiang Yu dies in battle, the scene shifts to Japan and the story of Kumagai no Naozane, Taira no Atsumori, and Princess Tamaori. Realizing the evanescence of life, Kumagai, who killed Atsumori, takes Buddhist orders. When he goes to the old battleground to visit the grave of Atsumori, he sees the fields blooming with masses of Yu poppies, so called after the Lady Yu of the Chinese story. He hears a flute. Atsumori's ghost appears and tells Kumagai that he wishes a green leaf flute to be placed as an offering in Kurotani Temple. The ghost of Princess Tamaori then appears, saying that she wants some of the red poppies blooming around the grave to be offered to the Buddha.

After this dance came a lively new one called "Kitano Elegance."

The dance of Kamishichiken was of the Hanayagi School, unlike Gion, which was of the Inoue.

After Takichiro left the Kitano Hall, he dropped in at the old-fashioned teahouse and plopped himself down in a seat. His manner prompted the proprietress to ask whom she might call for him.

"Hmm. How about the girl who bit the man's tongue? And also the girl in the blue kimono," Takichiro said.

"The girl on the train? Well, it would be all right if it's only for a greeting."

Takichiro had been drinking before the geisha arrived, so he purposely stepped outside. When the geisha came to accompany him, he asked, "Do you still bite?"

"You remember well. I won't bite. Stick out your tongue."

"I'm scared to."

"Really, I won't bite."

Takichiro stuck out his tongue. He felt the soft warmth inside.

He touched the girl's back lightly. "You've become quite depraved."

"Is this depravity?"

Takichiro wanted to gargle and rinse out his mouth, but he could not since the geisha was at his side.

He had made up his mind to do this bit of mischief with the geisha. Even to her it was a spur-of-the-moment act and had no real meaning. Takichiro did not dislike the geisha, nor did he think of her as dirty.

The geisha stopped him as he began to return to the parlor.

"Please wait," she said as she took out a handkerchief and

wiped Takichiro's mouth. There was lipstick on the handkerchief. The geisha brought her face closer to Takichiro, gazing at him. "Now, that's all right, isn't it?"

"Thank you." Takichiro placed both hands lightly on the geisha's shoulders.

The geisha stayed behind at the mirror in the rest room to touch up her own lipstick.

When Takichiro returned to the parlor no one was there. He had recovered slightly from the alcohol, so he drank two or three cups of cold sake as if to rinse his mouth.

Even so, the fragrance of the geisha—was it her perfume?—drifted in from somewhere. Takichiro felt vaguely young again.

Although the geisha's flirtation had been unexpected, he wondered if he had been cold toward her. Perhaps it was because he had not enjoyed himself with a young girl for a long time. This geisha of about twenty might turn out to be a particularly interesting woman.

The proprietress came in with the young girl. She was still wearing the long-sleeved blue kimono. "Since you requested, I asked her to come in to greet you. As you can see, she is quite young," the proprietress said.

Takichiro looked at the girl. "You served me tea a while ago."

"Yes." Being a girl of the teahouse, she was not shy. "When I brought the tea, I realized you were the man from the train."

"Oh, thank you. You remembered me?"

"Yes, I did."

When the geisha returned, the proprietress spoke to her. "Mr. Sada has taken quite a liking to this little girl."

"What?" The geisha looked at Takichiro's face. "You have a practiced eye, but you'll have to wait about three years. Besides, she's going to Pontocho next spring."

"Pontocho? Why?"

"She wants to be a *maiko*. She says she dreams of becoming a *maiko*."

"If she wants to be a *maiko*, wouldn't Gion be better?"

"Her aunt lives in Pontocho. That's why she's going there."

Takichiro gazed at the girl. She would become a first-rate *maiko* wherever she went.

The Nishijin Fabric Weavers Trade Association took an unprecedented measure by stopping all loom work for eight days from November twelfth until the nineteenth. Since the twelfth and the nineteenth were Sundays, it was actually only a six-day work stoppage.

There were a number of reasons, but, in short, the purpose was economic. They had overproduced and fabric on hand had grown to over three hundred thousand bolts. The purpose was to dispose of some of the stock and improve business. There had also been increasing problems in financing.

From the autumn of the previous year through the spring, some of the trading companies in Nishijin had folded.

It was said that by stopping work for eight days, stocks were reduced by some eighty or ninety thousand bolts. The results were favorable, so the strategy seemed to be a success.

As one could see from a glance at the streets in Nishijin, the weaving houses had followed the regulation, having a considerable amount of other fine handwork they could do in the shops.

The small houses, deep under the eaves of old weathered tile roofs, stood low side by side, as if lying prostrate. Even those with two stories were rather squat.

The alleys were like farm fields, but more disorderly. One could almost hear the sounds of the looms within the dusky darkness. Not all the looms were privately owned; some were rented.

They say only about thirty shops applied for exemption from the work stoppage.

Hideo's family did not make fabric; they wove obis. Naturally, they used electric lights as they worked at their three looms, even in the daytime, but their shop was much brighter than the average because there was open land in back. Still, the kitchen and furnishings were coarse, and one wondered where everyone in the house slept.

Hideo was persistent, blessed with a talent for his work and the diligence to go with it. He probably had bruises on his bottom from sitting continuously on the narrow slats of the loom.

When Hideo invited Naeko to see the Festival of Ages, the reason he was more taken by the green of the pines in spacious Gosho than by the parades of various period costumes was because it gave him an opportunity to escape from his everyday life. The scenery was not something that Naeko, who worked in the mountains and the narrow valleys, would have noticed particularly.

Having seen Naeko at the Festival of Ages wearing the obi he had woven, Hideo felt more encouraged in his work.

After Chieko went to Oichi with Ryusuke and Shin'ichi, she had moments when she felt as though she had lost her heart somewhere, though her feelings were not so severe as to be called suffering. When she noticed it, she thought it must be because of some anxiety.

On December thirteenth the Kotohajime passed, and the quickly changing winter weather of Kyoto began. The winter rain might sparkle in the sun even when the sky was cloudless. Occasionally sleet would fall, mixed with the rain. The sky would clear quickly, and quickly it would turn cloudy again.

New Year's preparations—in other words, the giving of year-end gifts—traditionally began after the Kotohajime. Naturally the place where this custom was observed most faithfully was the gay quarters. About that time the male attendants of the geisha and the *maiko* went about distributing rice cakes shaped like mirrors to the teahouses, the houses of Kabuki musicians, and the houses of the senior geisha—all who had been of assistance to the *maiko* and geisha.

Then the *maiko* went around making New Year's greetings. The purpose was to express thanks to those who had helped them in some way during the past year and to request their goodwill in the coming year. On this day, this "early new year," the comings and goings of the showily dressed *maiko* and geisha enlivened the atmosphere around Gion more than on any other day.

Chieko's shop was not nearly so festive.

After finishing breakfast, Chieko went upstairs alone to make herself up lightly, but her hands remained still.

Ryusuke's intense words at the soup shop in Kitano passed through Chieko's heart. It was a rather forceful way to put it, to say that he wished that Chieko had been abandoned in front of his shop when she was a baby.

Ryusuke's brother Shin'ichi was Chieko's childhood playmate and friend through high school. He had a gentle disposition, and although she knew that he liked her, Shin'ichi would never have said something that took away her breath the way Ryusuke had. She and Shin'ichi could enjoy one another's company without such worries.

Chieko combed her long hair, letting it hang down her back, then she went downstairs.

Just before breakfast was over, Chieko received a telephone call from the Kitayama village.

"Is this Miss Chieko?" Naeko asked. "I want to see you. Actually, I have something to tell you."

"Naeko, it's good to hear your voice. How would tomorrow be?" Chieko asked.

"Tomorrow is fine. Anytime."

"Please come to the shop," Chieko said.

"I'm sorry, but I'd rather not."

"It's all right. I've spoken to my mother, and my father knows about you, too."

"But the clerks are there."

Chieko thought for a moment. "Well, if that's the way you feel, I can meet you at your village."

"It's terribly cold here, but I'm so glad you'll come."

"I'd like to see the cedars anyway."

"Really? It's cold, and it may be drizzling, so be sure to dress for the weather. I can build a fire. I'll be working near the roadside so I'll know when you get here," Naeko said.

Winter Flowers

Chieko almost never wore slacks and a sweater, but today she did, along with heavy, brightly colored socks.

Since her father was at home, Chieko sat down to greet him. Takichiro looked wide-eyed at his daughter's unusual appearance. "Are you going walking in the mountains?"

"Yes . . . the girl from Kitayama said she wanted to see me today because she had something to talk about."

"I see." Takichiro showed no trace of hesitation. "Chieko."

"Yes?"

"If she has some problem or difficulty, please bring her home with you. We'll look after her."

Chieko looked down.

"It would be wonderful to have two daughters. Your mother and I would both be very happy."

"Thank you, Father. Thank you." Chieko bowed to him. Warm tears melted into her cheeks.

"Chieko, we've raised you since you were a nursing baby. You were the sweetest child anyone could hope for. We would treat that girl as fairly as possible. If she looks like you, she's surely a good girl. Bring her here. Twenty years ago twins weren't accepted, but now it's nothing," her father said. "Shige! Shige!" he called to his wife.

"Father, I understand. I think it would be wonderful, but Naeko will never come here to our house," Chieko said.

"Why is that?"

"It's probably because she doesn't want to be an obstacle to my happiness."

"Why would she think she'd be an obstacle?"

Chieko did not respond.

"Why would she think she'd be an obstacle?" he asked again, inclining his head.

"Even today, I asked her to come here to the shop, since you and mother already know about her." Chieko's voice was choked with tears. "She was afraid of trouble with the clerks or the neighbors."

"The clerks?" Takichiro's voice was unintentionally loud.

"I understand what you're thinking, but at least today I'm going to go see her."

"I see," her father nodded. "Take care. And it might be good if you'd tell that girl Naeko what I've just said."

"Yes, I will."

Chieko attached the hood to her raincoat. She wore galoshes over her shoes.

Though the sky over Nakagyo was clear, it might cloud over at any time. It could be drizzling or snowing at Kitayama; from within town it looked as if it were. But these were the small, gentle mountains of Kyoto, so snow would not necessarily enhance their beauty.

Chieko took the National Railway bus.

Two bus lines passed through Nakagawa Kitayama. The city bus turned around just before the mountain pass on the northern outskirts of the newly annexed portion of the city of Kyoto, but the National Railway bus ran all the way to Obama in Fukui Prefecture.

Obama was on the edge of Obama Bay, which opened into Wakasa Bay, which in turn opened out on the Sea of Japan.

Few passengers were on the bus, perhaps because it was winter.

A young man glared sharply at Chieko. He was accompanied by two other men. Feeling a vague apprehension, Chieko put up her hood.

"Miss, may I ask a favor? Please don't hide yourself like that." The man spoke in a hoarse voice not befitting his age.

"Hey, shut up," the man next to him said.

The man who spoke to Chieko was wearing handcuffs. What kind of criminal was he? Were the men beside him policemen? Where were they escorting this man, far beyond the deep mountains?

Chieko took down her hood, but she could not bring herself to show her face.

The bus had reached Takao.

"Where has Takao gone?" one passenger asked.

It did indeed look as though Takao had disappeared; the maple leaves had all fallen, and a touch of winter rested on the tips of the branches. The parking lot below Toganoo was empty.

Naeko had come out to the bus stop at Bodai Falls to wait for Chieko. She was in her work clothes.

For a moment, Naeko did not recognize Chieko in the outfit she was wearing.

"Thank you for coming. It's so remote here in the mountains."

"It's not that far." Chieko grasped Naeko's hands without removing her gloves.

"I'm so happy. I haven't seen you since summer. I had such a good time here."

"But I wondered what would have happened if we had been struck by lightning. Even so, I had such a good time then."

"Naeko," Chieko spoke as they walked down the road. "What you called about was urgent, wasn't it? I want you to tell me about it first. Can you talk about it calmly?"

Naeko did not speak. She wore her work clothes and a towel on her head.

"What is it?" Chieko asked.

"Actually . . . Hideo says he wants me to marry him. And . . . " Naeko stumbled. Chieko caught her as she reeled and held her.

Working hard every day as she did, Naeko's body was

strong and muscled. During the thunderstorm in the summer, Chieko had been frightened and had not noticed.

Naeko regained her composure, but she was happy that Chieko still held her. She did not tell her to stop. Instead she continued to lean on Chieko as she walked.

At the same time, Chieko began to lean on Naeko, but neither girl noticed.

Chieko had her hood up. "Naeko, what did you to say to Hideo?"

"My answer? I couldn't answer him on the spur of the moment."

Chieko did not speak.

"He mistook me for you—he knows the difference now—but, in his heart, deep down, you're the one there, Miss."

"No, that's not true."

"Yes, it is. I know quite well. Even if it's not a case of mistaken identity, it would be a vicarious marriage. In me, Hideo sees an illusion of you, Miss. That's the first problem," Naeko said.

Chieko recalled her mother reproving her father for asking what she would think of Hideo as a son-in-law when they were returning from the Botanical Garden on the bank of the Kamo River. The tulips had been in full bloom.

"And second, Hideo's shop makes obis, right?" Naeko said forcefully. "It would make trouble for you if I were somehow connected with your shop. People around you would look at you strangely. I couldn't make up for all the trouble I would cause you, even if I were to dare to try. I wish I could hide myself even further back in the mountains."

"Is that what you think?" Chieko shook Naeko's shoulders. "Today I told my father quite clearly I was coming to visit you, Naeko . . . and my mother knows, too . . ." Chieko shook Naeko all the harder. "What do you think my father said? . . . He said, 'If that girl Naeko needs help, bring her here. You are registered as my daughter, but as best I can, I'll be impartial and treat her well.' You're probably sad here all alone."

Naeko took the towel off her head. "Thank you." She rested her face in her hands. "I'm touched by your kindness. Thank you." For a moment Naeko could not speak.

"I've no one to turn to. I'm lonely, but I forget about it and work."

Chieko tried to lighten the mood. "The important thing is Hideo. What about him?"

"I can't answer him so quickly," Naeko said in a tearful voice as she looked at Chieko.

"Give me that." Chieko took Naeko's towel. "You can't go to the village crying like this." She wiped Naeko's eyes and face.

"I don't mind. I'm strong-willed, and I work my share, but I'm a crybaby."

When Chieko finished, Naeko put her face on Chieko's chest and sobbed convulsively.

"It's nothing to be troubled about, Naeko. Don't be sad." Chieko patted Naeko's back lightly. "If you're going to cry like that, I'll have to go home."

"No. No." Naeko was startled. Then she took her towel, which Chieko had been holding, and rubbed her own face roughly.

Since it was winter, one could not tell she had been crying except that the whites of her eyes were slightly red. Naeko put the towel on her head, concealing her face slightly.

The two did not speak for a moment.

After the limbs were cut, the round leaves were left behind on the top branches of the Kitayama cedars. To Chieko, these looked like plain green flowers of winter.

Sensing the moment was right, Chieko spoke to Naeko, "Hideo's obi designs are good, and he's a fine weaver."

"Yes, I know," Naeko answered. "When he invited me to

the Festival of the Ages, he was watching the colors reflecting from Higashiyama and the green pines at Gosho more than he was watching the parades of period costumes."

"The Festival of Ages is nothing unusual to him."

"No, that didn't seem to be it." Naeko put strength into her words. Chieko was silent, so she went on. "After the parade was finished, he invited me over."

"To his house?"

"Yes."

Chieko was slightly surprised.

"He has two younger brothers. He showed me the land behind the shop and said if we got married, he'd build a little place there and weave the things I liked."

"What's wrong with that?"

"What's wrong? I think Hideo wants to marry me as an illusion of you, Miss. I'm a girl. I know."

Chieko walked along, wondering what she might say.

In a small hollow off from the narrow valley, some elderly women who had been washing cedar logs were resting on an old car seat warming their hands and feet at a smoking fire.

Naeko passed in front of her own house, which was actually more of a hut. The straw thatch roof needed attention; it was leaning and almost seemed to wave. Being a mountain house, it had a small garden where red fruit hung from seven or eight tall nandina trees that grew in unattended disorder.

Perhaps this wretched hut had also been Chieko's.

Before they passed by the house, Naeko's thin tears had dried. Should she tell Chieko this was the house? Since Chieko was born in her mother's village, she had probably never been in this house. Even Naeko had no firm recollection of whether she had been here when she was an infant after losing her father and mother.

Fortunately, Chieko did not notice the house as she passed

by, gazing up at the uniformly aligned cedars. Naeko did not mention the hut.

Indeed, the round leaves left on the twigs of these straight trees were the "winter flowers" that Chieko fancied them to be.

Most of the houses were surrounded by cedar logs that had been washed, polished, and left standing side by side between the eaves and the second floor to dry. The white logs stood with their bases placed methodically in rows. Even that alone made them beautiful—perhaps more beautiful than any wall could be.

The uniform trees on the cedar mountains were also beautiful with dry grass at their bases. One could glimpse the sky through the spaces between the trunks.

"Isn't winter the most beautiful season?" Chieko asked.

"I wonder. I'm so used to seeing them, I don't know. Of course, in the winter the leaves take on the color of straw."

"That makes them look like flowers," Chieko said.

"Flowers? . . . Flowers?" Chieko's description was unexpected. Naeko looked up at the cedars.

As they walked they saw an elegant house. Did this belong to the landowners? The bottom half of the rather low wall was made from red painted boards, while the upper half was white. It had a small tile roof.

Chieko stopped. "This is a lovely house, isn't it?"

"Miss, this is the house where I'm staying. Please come in and look around. . . . They won't mind. They've taken care of me here almost ten years," Naeko said.

Chieko had heard Naeko say two or three times that Hideo wanted to marry her more because she was an illusion of Chieko than as her substitute.

Chieko could, of course, understand what she would mean by substitute. But what in the world did she mean by an "illusion," especially in reference to marriage?

"Naeko . . . illusion. You said, 'illusion.' But what do you mean?" Chieko said firmly.

Naeko did not answer.

"Isn't an illusion something without form that you can't touch with your hand?" Chieko continued, unexpectedly blushing. Naeko would belong to a man—this Naeko, who looked just like Chieko, not just in the face, but probably all over.

"Yes, that's right. That's what a formless illusion is," Naeko answered. "An illusion is in a man's heart, or mind . . . or maybe it dwells elsewhere, I don't know. Even when I'm an old woman of sixty, won't the Chieko of his illusion still be as young as you are now?"

Chieko did not expect such talk. "You've thought about it that much?"

"The time never comes when a beautiful illusion turns ugly."

"That's not necessarily true," Chieko finally said.

"You can't tread on an illusion."

"Hmm." Chieko could see envy even in Naeko. "Are there really such things as illusions?"

"In here . . . " Naeko touched Chieko's chest.

"I'm no illusion. I'm your twin."

Naeko did not speak.

"So won't you become my sister, at least with my spirit?"

"No, I want to be the sister of the Chieko before me. But, then . . . at least for Hideo's sake . . . "

"You think too much." Chieko looked down and walked for a moment. "Sometime, what if we talked together, the three of us, until we've settled things?"

"Talk? . . . Sometimes I want to . . . other times I don't."

"Naeko, are you so doubtful?"

"It's not that, but I have the heart of a young girl, too."

Naeko looked up. "The winter rain is coming down from Shuzan. Look at the cedars on the tops of the mountain."

Chieko lifted her eyes.

"Hurry home. It looks as though there will be sleet."

"I thought the weather might turn bad, so I brought some rain gear." Taking off one glove, Chieko showed her hand to Naeko. "This isn't the hand of a young 'Miss.'"

Naeko was startled. She wrapped her two hands around Chieko's.

Before Chieko realized it, it started drizzling. Although from these mountains, Naeko was caught unaware.

Chieko glanced around at the mountains. They appeared cold, shrouded in haze, but the trunks of the cedars at the foot of the slope looked all the clearer.

In a moment the small mountains became indistinct, as if wrapped in mist. It was different, of course, from the spring mist that descended from the sky, but perhaps this mist was more befitting Kyoto.

Looking at the ground, she realized it was damp.

As the mist surrounded them, the mountains were enveloped in a faint gray, which grew heavier and seemed to flow down the mountainside. Something white was mixed with the mist. It was sleet.

"You'd better hurry home," Naeko said when she noticed the white particles that vanished and reappeared.

The valley, which was dark for the time of day, suddenly turned cold. The rain was nothing unusual to a Kyoto girl like Chieko.

"You'd better hurry, before you turn into a cold illusion," Naeko said.

"Illusion? There you go again," Chieko laughed. "I came with rain gear. In Kyoto, the weather is always changing in the winter."

Naeko looked up at the sky. "You'd better go home now." She firmly grasped Chieko's ungloved hand.

"Naeko, are you really thinking about marriage?" Chieko asked.

"Just a little bit," Naeko answered. Then she lovingly put the glove back on Chieko's hand.

"Please come to my house once," Chieko said, but Naeko did not respond.

"Please come . . . after the clerks have gone home."

"At night?" Naeko was surprised.

"You can stay over. My father and mother know all about you."

Naeko's eyes filled with joy, but she hesitated.

"At least once I want you to sleep in the same room with me."

Naeko looked to the far side of the road, and before Chieko knew it, Naeko was crying. Chieko could nt avoid noticing.

When Chieko returned home to Muromachi, it was only cloudy there.

"You got home just in time, before it starts raining," her mother, Shige, said. "Your father's waiting for you in the back."

Before Chieko had finished greeting her father, he asked eagerly, "How did it go, Chieko, when you talked to her?"

"Well . . . " Chieko puzzled over what she should say. It would be difficult to explain clearly in a few words.

"How was it?" he asked again.

"Well . . . "

Chieko had understood what Naeko had said, but there were also some things that she could not comprehend. Hideo really wanted to marry Chieko, but he had given that up as impossible, saying instead he wanted to marry Naeko, Chieko's twin. Naeko's young heart discerned his feelings, so she told Chieko about her strange "illusion" theory.

Did Hideo intend to forbear his desire for Chieko by taking

Naeko? Chieko did not think it was merely conceit that made her feel it was true.

But perhaps that was not all.

Chieko could not look at her father's face directly; even the sinews in her neck seemed to betray her feeling of awkwardness.

"So this Naeko just wanted to see you?" her father asked.

"Yes," Chieko resolutely raised her head. "She said that Otomo's son Hideo wants to marry her." Chieko's voice quavered.

"Hmm?" Her father watched her and for a moment he was silent. He seemed to be looking at something beyond, but he did not speak.

"So . . . Hideo. It would be good if she married a boy like Hideo. Fate is certainly a strange thing, but then maybe it's all thanks to you."

"But, Father, I don't think she'll marry Hideo."

"What? Why not?"

Chieko did not answer.

"Why not? It seems all right to me."

"You're right. It wouldn't be bad, but, Father, do you remember at the Botanical Garden, when you asked how Hideo would be as a match for me? That girl knows all about that."

"Really? How?"

"She thinks that Hideo's shop and ours have at least some business dealings."

This echoed in Takichiro's chest. He fell silent.

"Father, once would be enough, but please could Naeko come here to stay just one night. Please."

"Of course . . . But why are you asking? I told you we would even take her in permanently, didn't I?"

"But she would never come here to live. Only for a night."

Her father looked at her compassionately.

They heard the sound of Shige closing the rain shutters.

"I'll go help." Chieko stood up.

The almost inaudible touch of winter rain sounded on the roof. Chieko's father sat motionless.

Takichiro was invited to dinner by the father of Ryusuke and Shin'ichi at Saami in Maruyama Park. The winter days were short, so the city lights were already visible from the heights of the parlor. The sky was gray, with no evening glow. Except for the lights, the town itself was also gray—the color of the Kyoto winter.

Mizuki Ryusuke's father was a strong dependable personality, being the owner of a large Muromachi wholesale house that had prospered considerably, but today he seemed to have difficulty expressing himself. He hesitated, spending time talking of trivial gossip.

"Actually," he finally spoke up, after borrowing some nerve from the sake. Takichiro was a passive man who tended toward pessimism. This was enough for him to guess the purpose of Mizuki's talk.

"Actually," Mizuki seemed about to stumble on his words again. "Has your daughter said anything about my son Ryusuke?"

"Yes. . . . Our house could hardly be worthy of such consideration, but I understand Ryusuke's good intentions."

"I see." Mizuki seemed to be more at ease. "He's much like I was when I was young. Once he says it, it doesn't matter who tries to stop him, he won't listen. He's a problem."

"No, I'm very grateful to him."

"I'm relieved to hear you say so," Mizuki said, appearing genuinely relieved. "Please forgive me," he bowed politely.

Though Takichiro's shop was having financial difficulties, it would be a disgrace to have a mere boy come in to help out, particularly one from a similar business. Still he could not pretend he came to learn since the two shops were of opposite styles.

"I'm thankful, but . . . " Takichiro said. "You can't do without Ryusuke at your shop."

"What? Ryusuke just observes the business. He doesn't know much. He doesn't listen to what his parents tell him, but he's a diligent boy."

"Yes, I was quite surprised when he came to my shop. He sat down in front of one of my clerks and gave him some quite harsh looks."

"That's the kind of boy he is," Mizuki said. He drank more sake in silence. "Mr. Sada."

"Yes."

"If Ryusuke could go to your shop to assist you—not necessarily every day—I think it would help his brother Shin'ichi become more responsible, and that would be a help to me, too. Shin'ichi is a gentle boy. Even now Ryusuke often teases him, calling him 'the little festival boy.' That's the worst thing. It's from when he was on the float in the Gion Festival."

"It's because he's so pretty. He's been friends with Chieko since they were children."

"About Chieko . . . " Again Mizuki was at a loss for words. "About Chieko," he repeated. He sounded as if he were angry. "How did such a good and beautiful girl come to be?"

"It wasn't through her parents' efforts. She just turned out that way," Takichiro answered directly.

"I suppose you understand, Mr. Sada. Your business is similar to mine, and the reason Ryusuke says he wants to help at your shop is so he can be by Chieko's side for even thirty minutes or an hour a day."

Takichiro nodded. Mizuki wiped his forehead.

"He's not much of a son, but he works hard. I don't want to ask the impossible, but if by some chance Chieko should decide someday that a fellow like Ryusuke would be suitable, and if you were to agree to it, well . . . it's rather brazen of me to ask, but if that were the case, could I ask you to take him in as an adopted son-in-law? I would disinherit him so he could marry into your family." He lowered his head.

"Disinherit him? Your successor?"

"That's not what brings people happiness. That's what I think when I look at Ryusuke nowadays."

"Your intentions are kind, but let's leave it up to the two of them. They're young." Takichiro avoided Mizuki's severity. "And Chieko was a foundling."

"What do you mean, a 'foundling'?" Mizuki asked. "Well . . . please keep in mind what I've said. May I send Ryusuke to your shop as an assistant?"

"Yes."

"Thank you. Thank you." Mizuki's body seemed to relax. Even his manner of drinking changed.

The next morning when Ryusuke came to Sada's shop, he quickly gathered the clerks together to take inventory. He just watched, saying nothing. Since Ryusuke's last visit, the head clerk had been shy of him; he did not even lift his head.

The Sadas tried to get Ryusuke to stay longer, but he left before supper.

That evening there was a loud knocking at the lattice door, but only Chieko heard. It was Naeko.

"Oh, Naeko, you came . . . and it's so cold this evening." Naeko did not speak.

"But the stars are out."

"Chieko, would it be all right if I met your parents?"

"I've told them all about you, so all you'll have to say is, 'I'm Naeko.'" Chieko hugged Naeko's shoulders as she walked to the back of the house with her. "Have you had supper?"

"Yes, thank you. I had some sushi just before I came."

Naeko's manner was formal. Chieko's parents were so astounded by the two girls' resemblance that they could not speak.

"Go on upstairs in the back. The two of you make yourselves at home and talk." Shige was the one finally able to express herself.

Chieko took Naeko's hand as they crossed the narrow veranda, went upstairs, and lit the heater.

"Naeko, come here a moment," Chieko called her to the dressing mirror. Chieko stared at their two faces.

"We certainly do look alike." Chieko felt a hot rush enter her body. They changed sides. "We're really the very images of each other."

"That's what twins are," Naeko said.

"What would happen if everyone had twins?"

"People would always be mistaking one another. It would certainly cause problems." When Naeko stepped back, her eyes were moist. "One can never know fate."

Chieko stepped toward Naeko and grasped her shoulders firmly. "Naeko, couldn't you stay here always? Father and Mother have said they want you to. I'm very lonely here by myself. Maybe the cedar mountains are a pleasant place, but . . ."

Naeko seemed unable to remain standing. Kneeling down as if otherwise she might stagger, she shook her head. Teardrops fell on her knees.

"Miss, our lives and our upbringing have been different. I couldn't live in a place like Muromachi. Once, just this once, I've come to your home. I wanted to show you the kimono you gave me. . . . And you were kind enough to come visit me twice in the cedar mountains."

Chieko was silent, so Naeko continued, "Miss, you are the one that our parents abandoned. I don't know why."

"But I've forgotten that," Chieko said without pausing. "I don't even think of it. It's as though I never had any such parents."

"I think . . . maybe both of them have received their punishment. I was just a baby, but please forgive me."

"What kind of sin, what kind of responsibility could you have?"

"It's not that. I told you before I don't want to be even the slightest obstacle to your happiness." Naeko lowered her voice. "I'd rather disappear completely."

"No, don't say that." Chieko spoke firmly. "It seems so unfair. Naeko, are you unhappy?"

"No, I'm lonely."

" 'Good fortune is short, while loneliness is long.' Isn't that true?" Chieko asked. "Let's lie down. I want to talk some more." Chieko took the bedding from the closet. Naeko helped her.

"Happiness. This is happiness." Naeko was listening to a sound coming from the roof.

Seeing Naeko straining to hear, Chieko stood motionless and asked, "Is it winter rain? Or sleet? Or both?"

"Maybe. Or is it snow?"

"Snow?"

"It's quiet. Hardly enough to call snow . . . just a fine powder. In the mountain village sometimes a snow like this comes while we're working and before we know it, the surfaces of the leaves turn white like flowers . . . and even the tips of the fine twigs of the dead winter trees."

Chieko listened.

"Sometimes it stops, or turns to sleet or a winter rain."

"Shall we open the shutter and see? We'll know right away." Chieko got up, but Naeko held her back.

"Don't! It's cold, and besides it would destroy the illusion."

"Illusion? Did you say 'illusion'? You talk about illusions quite a bit."

Naeko smiled. There was a faint sorrow about her beautiful face.

Naeko hurriedly spoke as Chieko was about to spread out the futon. "Chieko, just this once let me prepare your bedding for you."

Chieko got into her futon. The two lay side by side.

"Oh, Naeko, it's so warm."

"Our labor is different . . . just like the places we live."

Naeko embraced Chieko. "It will be cold on a night like this," Naeko said, as if she were not the least bit chilled. "Tonight the powder snow will drift down . . . stop . . . then flutter down again."

Takichiro and Shige came upstairs to the next room. Being older, they used an electric blanket to warm the bed.

Naeko whispered in Chieko's ear, "Your bed is warm now so I'll get into mine."

Later, Chieko's mother opened the sliding door a crack to peep into the girls' room.

The next morning, Naeko got up very early. She shook Chieko to awaken her. "Miss, this has been the happiest time of my life. I'm going to leave now before anyone sees me."

Just as Naeko had said, a light powder snow had been falling off and on during the night. Now the cold morning glistened.

Chieko got up. "You don't have a raincoat do you? Here, take this." She got out her best velvet coat, a collapsible umbrella, and high clogs for Naeko.

"These are for you. Come again . . . please."

Naeko shook her head. Chieko stood against the Bengara lattice door, watching as Naeko walked away. Naeko did not look back. A few delicate snowflakes fell on Chieko's hair and quickly vanished.

The town was as it should be, still silent in sleep.

Design by David Bullen
Typeset in Mergenthaler Caslon Old Face #2
with Cochin Display
by Wilsted & Taylor
Printed by Haddon Craftsmen
on acid-free paper